Matthew David Evans

Black Rose Writing

www.blackrosewriting.com

First printing

ISBN: 978-1-61296-057-9

PUBLISHED BY BLACK ROSE WRITING

www.blackrosewriting.com

Printed in the United States of America

Prophets of the Otherworld is printed in Andalus

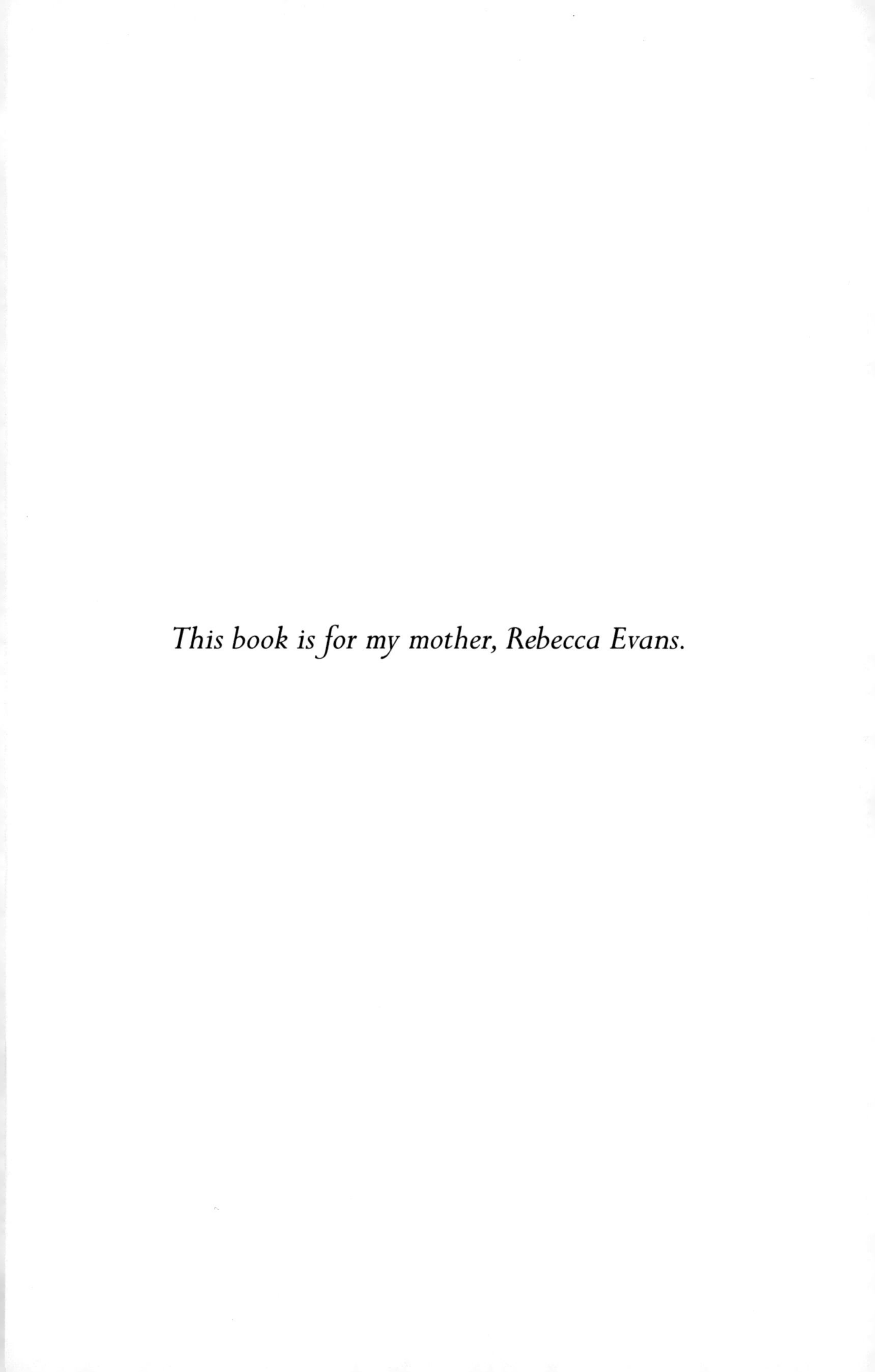

This book is for my mother, Rebecca Evans.

Prophets
of the
Otherworld

Chapter One

For centuries, the Otherworld has been at war. The disappearance of the Gods sparked an eternal unrest that affected all who crossed the River of Souls. All who died went to a heaven turned into hell by civil war.

Dying was just fine as far as Lord Percival was concerned. He lay in the darkness of his bed chambers in his hall, Cadan Mol. The room that once felt so lively and bright now had a dark feeling of decay about it. The stone floors were dirty, the bed was soiled and Percival himself had lost all control of his bladder. Lying in a constant puddle of piss, he wanted to growl for his servants to clean him. His pride would not let him. Let me lie here and die, he thought. Damn the lot of them.

This was not a true sentiment that he felt but merely the frustrations of becoming a feeble old man. He was once a great lord governing the largest portion of the kingdom of Armora. He had been a favorite of three generations of the monarchs. His great anger came when he thought about how he was failing his king and queen by lying in his own urine as hordes of invaders were undoubtedly camping on the boarders of the kingdom. It was not the responsibility of Percival's commanders, or his sons to keep the enemies at bay. It was his. It was charged to him but now he couldn't possibly hope to complete his task. The grandfather of the present king had appointed him to this position after he had shown great strength and leadership in battle. In fact, those battles in which Percival marched with the king, he had glutted the ground with the blood of enemies. He had been one of the most ferocious men in the kingdom, but now what was he? He was a dying old man who hadn't strength enough to lift his sword let alone charge into battle on horseback.

What would old King Morlon think if he saw me now?

But there was another voice in Percival's mind arguing that King Morlon would be astounded at how long Percival had lived. Sixty-five years was an astounding lifespan. Few made it past forty-five. Morlon had only lived to be forty-seven. His son, King Rylan had died at thirty years of age, but that was in battle. That left child king Taringor in charge at the age of twelve. Now Taringor was twenty-seven years old and in the prime of his life. The thought angered Percival whenever he thought of it. He quickly turned the anger around on himself for even having the audacity to covet the king.

But damn it, why not? My years are coming to an end and he's got years of health ahead of him. Why shouldn't I want that?

He would always berate himself for thinking such things. It was all about death with him. He was afraid to face it. And why shouldn't he be? No one knew what was beyond the River of Souls. What if it was hellfire and torment? What if it was nothing at all? What if the Gods set up for him torments at the hands of his slain enemies? Would he be their slave? He had always told his men that slain enemies would be their slaves in the Otherworld, but what if he himself became a slave? His fear was far too great to think rationally anymore. He wanted his youth back. He wanted to postpone the journey over the River. He wanted to live damn it. Oh, how he wanted to live.

Stupid old fool. He knew that wasn't true. He was tired of his life. He was tired of being a warrior. Even now as he lay in decrepitude he knew he was still a warrior. This was the first time in years he had allowed himself to look back on his life and really ponder how he had gotten to that point. He could fight and so he did. That made him a warrior. He remembered years earlier wanting to be a scholar. He had learned his letters and was growing knowledgeable of history and science.

Then war came.

He had been the son of a farmer when Armora was invaded by the barbarian Pastons. Percival had acquired a sword and shield and had fought alongside his brothers to defend his homeland. Percival joined up with Caltrin, the warlord magician and champion of the king. Caltrin led a great campaign against the Pastons and he and Percival had fought side by side and back to back. During that war, Percival had become a hero. When his brothers returned to the farm, Percival stayed in Caltrin's warband.

It was a living, Percival had thought. He had stayed behind and learned how to be a soldier for it seemed a way to become rich. Once he became rich, he thought, he could spend all the time he wanted researching and studying anything that interested him. He spent years among the warband, learning how to fight. He had already known the basics of fighting with a sword but Caltrin taught him to be a proper soldier. He became a great warrior very fast and eventually earned the title of warlord.

It was not long after he had earned the title of warlord that Caltrin had been slain in battle. The wizard's magical scepter had become fractured and the power was drained. He was cut down by an enemy.

The mourning for Caltrin was felt throughout Armora. The people had thought that with the magician on their side that they were invincible. Now they felt vulnerable.

Percival was chosen as the champion of the king after Caltrin had been killed. Finally, Percival had wealth and power, but he could not begin his life as a scholar. He had greater responsibilities. There would be no hanging up the sword for him for he would constantly be at war with someone. He had spent the remainder of his youth and all of his middle-age as a champion, never having lived the way he wanted.

"Perhaps when I die," Percival said to himself, "I can finally do what I want to do. I can finally hang up the sword."

A horn sounded. He heard the faint whisper of arrows cutting through the air. The sun was setting and an orange glow was illuminating the bedchamber. He looked toward his windows along the castle wall. The sky and become purple and he could see individual rays of light. He wondered if the Otherworld would be like this. He hoped it would. This was the first time in his life that he ever truly appreciated a sunset. Perhaps it was because this could be the last he ever saw or maybe he just felt that it resembled the sun setting on his life. Either way, he knew he liked it.

He saw, through the orange rays, a dark figure soaring toward him. It wasn't until it was in the bedchamber that he recognized it as a crow. It sat perched upon his bedpost and gazed into his eyes. Percival held out a hand.

"Hello, my friend," he said in a raspy whisper.

The crow cawed and flapped its wings but did not fly away. It resumed its gaze. Percival stared back. He was beginning to doze but feared not waking. He kept his eyes locked on the crow, feeling that in some way this bird was letting him know that he would be dead before the sun set. As he realized this, the bird launched from the bedpost and flew out the window. Percival had a brief moment of envy for the crow. After all the bird was free while Percival was caged by his own body. There was realization that he would not wake in the morning, he would probably not even go to sleep again. He had to speak with his household one last time. He resolved to call his sons and servants into the bedchamber.

He roared for his servants to come to him. He knew that they were out there. He had servants just beyond the door waiting to hear an order from him. If they did not hear from him once an hour, they would send someone in to check on him. This was a hassle at night when he would sleep as he would have to leave the door open for the doctors to come in and out to make sure he still lived. More times than not, when they checked on him, they woke him.

"Come here!" he called.

He had dropped all formalities weeks ago and was merely bellowing his orders in their raw form. It was to no one in particular, just to whoever might be within earshot. Sure enough, three servants came into his room. Percival noticed that none were doctors but decided it best not to waste his remaining energy on calling the doctors in to berate them.

"You," he said pointing to the servant closest to him. She was a short dirty haired woman with several holes in her smile. She hadn't bathed in weeks, but even she recoiled at the stench of the bedchambers as she cautiously approached the dying warlord.

"Yes, my lord?" she asked.

"I forget names… Servant One," Percival said. "Send for my sons. Tell them to hurry."

"Yes, lord," she nodded and turned to leave.

"Time is short," Percival called after her. "Time is short."

The other two servants remained, waiting to see if their lord required anything from them. Percival stared into their eyes just as the crow had stared into his.

"You smell that?" he asked.

They nodded silently. Both were obviously ashamed that they had let their lord's last days be filled with such squalor.

"What do you have to say about it?" Percival hissed.

They exchanged nervous glances and looked absently to the

ground. Seeing their shame and humiliation, Percival laughed. An old man dying in his own shit was allowed to be an ass.

"Just in case you're wondering," Percival said. "You cannot go. I have something to say and you two may as well hear it. Until then... breathe in! Ha!"

Though the servants tried their hardest, Percival could detect a hint of displeasure at this revelation. They seemed to desperately want to leave. They would soon enough.

Time is short.

The crow danced in his memory for the few minutes they were waiting. He saw the beautiful creature fly through the window. He saw its deep black eyes. He felt the way he felt when he realized that the crow was a death omen. How could he have even momentarily forgotten that? His earliest lessons as a boy were how to read omens. There were everywhere and they gave the most important warnings. To Percival, forgetting your omens was like forgetting your shield when you went to battle. It's as if you're asking to die.

The servant returned, interrupting Percival's self scolding. Behind her were Percival's two sons.

"The lords Gelvin and Arhamor," the servant said, bowing her head. She effectively masked her disgust at the smell.

"Thank you," Percival said.

He lay there regarding his two sons for a long while. He had a fleeting thought of the fact that neither had yet married. This was strange as they were in their thirties. They had better do it soon or his line would end. Then he thought about how absurd that was. Who cared if his line ended? He wouldn't know about it. Or would he?

The two men waited patiently for their father to speak. Gelvin the oldest, unlike his father and brother, had grown a full beard. It was shaggy, covered half of his face and stretched down his torso. It looked odd in contrast with his short hair. He was a warrior. How good a warrior was he though? Could he possibly be expected to keep the enemy at bay for years to come? Perhaps King Taringor would appoint a new lord for this manor. It was one of the most important spots in the kingdom, and not just any lord could rule it. Gelvin's sword was tightly clasped in his scabbard. Percival thought about how that sword could potentially be replaced by his own before tomorrow.

Arhamor idly scratched at the stump of his left arm where a hand used to be. He had lost it while defending the village against a raid. Percival remembered the incident. There hadn't been any choice in the matter. Arhamor's hand had been trapped under a burning wagon and the raiders were closing in. Percival did the only logical thing without hesitation. The memory of it still occasionally haunted their dreams. Percival had raised his sword and brought the heavy blade down on his son's wrist. It had taken only one strike. Blood had gushed from the wound but they were able to get behind a shield-wall and bind the it before too much blood could be lost. Despite all of this, Arhamor had remained a formidable soldier. He couldn't do archery anymore but he could still wield a sword. When in battle, both Arhamor and Gelvin sent scores of men across the River of Souls. They were almost as good as Lord Percival.

"My sons," Percival wheezed.

Both men were thinking about how far their father had fallen in a year. It was the damned sickness that had started it. No doctor or magician that they brought into the manor could do anything for him. It was as if despite all treatments he was destined for this. The grimmest of truths is that there is no cure for destiny.

"We are here, Father," Gelvin said.

"My time is short," Percival said before beginning a coughing fit.

Gelvin turned to the servants. "Get water in here now," he said.

"Hang the water!" Percival said through his coughs. "Listen to me."

Gelvin and Arhamor moved closer to the bed. They did not recoil from the stench. Arhamor did plan on punishing whoever was not taking proper care of his father.

"My time is short," Percival said. "I have been told this."

"How, Father?" Arhamor interrupted.

Percival inhaled deeply and Gelvin shot a dark look at his brother.

"I received an omen," Percival said. "Anything else you want to say, or should I continue?"

"Continue Father," Arhamor said looking embarrassed.

"When I am dead," Percival began, "the raiders will come, you know this. I want a messenger dispatched to the king to inform him of my death because when that happens, our enemies may be emboldened. We'll need more spearmen.

"Gelvin, I know you feel it is your responsibility and birthright to protect the manor but the king may select someone else for this job. You cannot become angry about it because it is a dangerous and tiresome task, keeping this border secure. Go where your king commands, not where your sentimentality directs.

"Arhamor. Sorry again about you hand. You're stronger than I was at your age. I know that for a time, my hall is in good hands. Please, Arhamor and you as well, Gelvin, find a woman and continue the line. My time is almost done but I would like some hope of having descendants carrying on for years after me."

Percival broke into a nasty coughing fit, one that made all others that had come before it look healthy. After a few coughs it was no longer phlegm he was spewing into his hands, but blood.

"What do we do, Gelvin?" Arhamor asked panicking. He turned to the servants. "Do something!" he ordered.

Percival held up a hand to stop them.

"It's over," he said through his bloody coughs.

He exhaled one last time and was gone.

Arhamor and Gelvin leaned closer and watched the life leave their father's eyes. They looked no different now than they had when he was alive and yet there was a great contrast between then and now. They had the look of death, of hollowness.

"I can't believe he's actually gone," Arhamor said at last, laying his remaining hand on Percival's forehead.

Gelvin was speechless. He had accepted that this would happen. It seemed a necessary evil. Few men lived as long as Percival had. Few were still able to fight at that age. Percival had been able to fight up until the point when sickness overcame him. He had led spearmen in a defense not a year earlier. Until the sickness had come, no man would draw a sword against him without thinking twice.

Gelvin turned toward the servants. "I want him cleaned. I want his room cleaned up and his bedding… and bring his sword."

The servants got started right away.

"Bring his sword?" Arhamor asked.

"This is Lord Percival," Gelvin said. "He should be honored here before his burial."

It took hours. First the corpse of Lord Percival was moved off of the bed and onto a cart and taken out of the bedchamber to be cleaned. The remaining servants scrubbed the room and the bedding. They got rid of all traces of the smells of waste. Percival's wolf banner was propped up at one side of the bed while the horse standard of Armora was propped on the other.

Percival was cleaned and redressed in his armor, all except for his helmet. Then he was put into his bed with his sword clasped in his hands, pointing toward his feet.

Arhamor and Gelvin were the only ones remaining in the room once the servants had finished their work. It seemed to both of them that they had an obligation to mourn until the dawn. This was not a custom by any means but something inside of them told them it was the right thing to do. The captains of the spearmen could patrol the border for tonight. Tonight the two heirs of Cadan Mol mourned the passing of Lord Percival.

Chapter Two

The River of Souls has existed since the formation of the worlds. It is a winding body of water separating the mortal world from the Otherworld. Its name is derived not only from the souls who cross on the great ships but also for the disembodied souls who haunt the waves in eternal maddened torment.

Percival was no longer in pain. He felt disoriented and dazed for a moment and then realized he was standing. He was standing next to the bed. He was standing next to his corpse.

There was a bright light that washed over all the room. He looked out the window and saw that everything was washed in the strange light. He marveled at the sight for a moment and then noticed that his new body was now forming. It was not the frail body of his old age that formed but a youthful body. He felt hair growing rapidly on his face and head and felt his lungs fill with air as he began to breathe.

He looked at his sons. They did not seem to notice him. Indeed, they could not see him. Gelvin wept and took the sword in his hands. Percival would not be buried with the sword for it was the custom to pass the sword to the eldest son. Gelvin was now the ruler of this hall, until the king said otherwise.

Percival heard a horn sound and looked out the window again. He saw that where there had been fields and woodland, there was now a body of water. It had appeared just as Percival's new body had appeared. On this body of water was a boat. The sight of the boat made Percival's heart leap with joy and sink with fear at the same time. He knew what that boat was. It was Barwick's ship. Barwick was the boatman known for taking dead souls to the Otherworld. Percival wondered absently whether the boatman's name really was Barwick or if that had been a name that the holy men of Armora had created. The ship was unlike anything Percival had ever seen. It was a long, wooden vessel that had no sails. There were no openings for oars on the sides and Percival couldn't see how the ship could move.

Percival left Cadan Mol and walked at a brisk pace toward the ship. As he approached he grew aware that though his new body had formed, no clothing had formed with it. He slowed as he realized this but then shook his head and continued at the pace he was going.

There was a man standing on the shore. He was tall and broad-shouldered. He was cloaked in brown and every part of him was covered except for his pale face which bore a black scar on the right cheek.

"Percival," the man said. "Come along. It's time you crossed."

"Yes, it is," Percival said.

"My name is Barwick and I will be guiding this boat to the Otherworld. Your cabin is number twelve. You will find clothes and food there."

Percival looked at the boat and saw that there was no ramp to climb aboard. There was no ladder either.

"How do I climb aboard?" he asked.

Barwick waved his hand lazily and he and Percival both vanished an reappeared on the boat. Barwick was on the deck while Percival appeared in cabin number twelve.

"Prepare for immediate departure," Barwick's voice magically echoed through the ship.

Percival put on a cloak that was lying on a chest and then lay down in a hammock. He felt the ship begin to move and felt a tremor of excitement as it set off across the river.

After a short time, Percival got off the hammock and opened the chest which was the only piece of furniture in the cabin. Inside was a pile of fruit and vegetables. He realized for the first time since he died that he was very hungry. He ate greedily, shoving grapes into his mouth and ripping into the skin of the apples. Fruit juices ran down his newly grown beard. There was also a jar of water in the chest and Percival drained it and marveled as the jar refilled instantly.

His appetite and thirst satisfied, Percival left his cabin to explore more of the ship. The workings of the ship intrigued him. The magic that he had so far experienced was mesmerizing. He wanted to talk to Barwick and learn how the magic was used.

He climbed stairs at the end of the hall and opened a door. He saw that he was standing on the deck of the ship. All around, the world looked different than anything he had seen. The sky was green and there were clouds gathering to blot out the moonlight. The water was a rippling sea in turmoil. Percival still could not see any logical way that the ship could be moving and resolved himself to the fact that it was more magic.

"Couldn't resist exploring, eh?" Barwick said from his position at the wheel.

"No," Percival said. "It's amazing."

Barwick laughed and left the wheel to guide itself, which it did. He plucked Percival's arm and led him to the front of the deck. "Tell me what you see," Barwick said.

"I see water and small pockets of mist," Percival replied.

"And what can you hear?"

Percival listened for a moment. He heard the water splash onto the hull and heard something that sounded like rowing and guessed that there really were oars rowing the boat but they were invisible. Then he heard a faint moaning sound. He listened harder and could hear more moaning and some screaming. "What is that?" he asked.

"The truly dead," Barwick replied. "When someone dies in the Otherworld, that person becomes a ghost. His mortal body is dead and his other body is destroyed. There is no where else for the soul to go. It ends up here on the River."

"That's awful."

"Indeed," Barwick said. "The Gods didn't finish their work before they vanished. Dead souls grow thicker on the river. Some have even begun escaping into the mortal world. This causes a lot of problems."

"But they're just spirits. They can't harm mortals right?"

"They can affect things to an extent. The souls are maddened, you see? They experience great pain being disembodied for so long and end up as screaming wraiths. This is the true afterlife."

"But why?" Percival asked. "Why did the Gods make it this way?"

"It was long ago. The Gods no longer have control of it. The thing that rules the Otherworld now floods the river with these spirits."

"And who rules the Otherworld?" Percival asked.

"Serpintus does. The minion overlord. He's ruled for millennia."

"And the Gods let this happen?"

"The Gods abandoned humanity after humanity sided with the minions. How humanity mourns that great mistake."

"That's awful," Percival said again.

Just then the ship passed through a cluster of mist and Percival felt terror grip his heart as he heard the cries of agony coming from the spirits.

"Some of them don't even remember their lives," Barwick said. "Some are no longer aware of their existence. It is, as you said, awful."

Percival walked back toward the cabins, leaving Barwick

standing where he was. "Is it a river or a sea?" Percival asked.

"It's a river that is so wide in places that it seems like a sea. We have already crossed over into the Otherworld but I have a special place where I will be dropping you."

"Is there anyone else on the ship?"

"Of course there is! What a question!. Come now man. More than you have died."

"I don't understand though. How can you possibly pick up everyone who dies?"

Barwick sighed. It seemed he was asked this very question a lot. "I have special powers since I have this position," he said. "I can multiply myself and my ships to the number needed. Right now there are fifteen of me and fifteen of my ships carrying dead souls across the river."

"Fifteen?"

"Yes. It is a power that only I have since only I take souls across the river. No one understands this except me, so don't even bother trying to figure it out. It's just the way it's been for a thousand years."

"Okay then," Percival said.

"Listen," Barwick said, "I would like to talk to you later, but I have some work to do now. I'll see you soon. It's very important."

With that, Barwick snapped his fingers and vanished. Percival looked around and saw no one on the deck. He shrugged and went through the door once again and walked back down the stairs and headed for cabin number twelve. He had not had many questions answered and had actually discovered new ones. This world of magic frightened the former warlord who preferred to rely on his sword and shield and spear. Magic was not reliable. Caltrin's death had proved that. Things were different now however. He was in the Realm of the Gods even if those Gods were gone. He was in the Otherworld.

Percival looked forward to having an afterlife devoid of conflict.

He had spent his entire life as a warrior and it seemed as though he was always at war with someone. Now he could spend his time studying like he always wanted to do in life. It was true that he knew more than the average lice-ridden thuggish brutes whom he stood shoulder to shoulder with in shield-walls but he was a fool compared to the wise men he respected so much. There were many things to study in the Otherworld and at the top of the list was the magic which seemed to govern what he had seen so far. He felt absurdly optimistic about being able to do this and didn't take into account the bad things that Barwick had told him about Serpintus and the tyranny ruling the Otherworld. He felt he could find a quiet corner in eternity and simply exist. He would bother no one and no one would bother him. He had thought about this during the time he talked with Barwick on the deck and he thought about it as he walked back to his cabin. Once inside cabin twelve however, something happened that made Percival fear for his dream future. When he opened his door, he noticed a man standing in his room. He did not know the man and merely thought that the stranger had entered the wrong cabin. In truth, the man did not enter the wrong cabin. He had come to talk with the former warlord. And so it was that Percival met the prophet Norhan for the first time.

Norhan was a man of medium height who constantly wore a grave expression on his face. He was clad in a brown cloak similar to the one Percival wore and had overgrown hair and an overgrown beard. Percival supposed everyone looked similar when they received their new bodies. Percival looked into Norhan's eyes and Norhan stared back with grim determination.

"Sir, I believe this is my cabin," Percival said.

"Indeed," Norhan replied.

"Then may I ask why you are here?"

"I have something to say to you," Norhan said.

"You may say it," Percival replied. "But first tell me who you are."

"I am called Norhan."

"The prophet," Percival said. He had heard of Norhan. In fact, most of the kingdom had heard of Norhan. The prophet was a legend and Percival had not heard of his death. That was no real surprise however since he had received little news in his final weeks of life.

"The prophet," Norhan nodded. "A great power in life that seems to have continued into death. I am guided to speak to you and I ask that you listen for it makes my task that much easier."

"Then speak," Percival said.

"You believe yourself free of war and free of fighting. Fate has decreed otherwise. You will be a great force, a warrior of the Gods. You are indeed destined to be a champion of the Gods. Your death shall mirror your life and you will spend time in agony. It is through the darkness you will go and because of the darkness you must fight. You are to be the leader in the final wars and these wars shall wage through the ages. Your desires will be elusive, but you will know a victory through a great defeat."

"Is that it?" Percival said.

"It is," Norhan replied.

Percival nodded. He heard prophets talk like this before. In his life he was told he was going to be instrumental in the final wars but every war he fought seemed only to create another war. He was not an instrument of war and he did not believe in Fate. He would make his own existence despite what this prophet said.

"Thank you for that, Norhan," Percival said. "Now if you don't mind, I would like to sleep."

Norhan nodded and left the cabin. Percival lay in the hammock and drifted off to sleep. He paid no mind to what Norhan had said. He had heard before that Norhan was mad and now believed the rumors. Who would barge into a stranger's cabin and proclaim a horrid prophecy? He was glad to see Norhan go and vowed not to talk to that man again should he happen across him during the remainder of the voyage.

A couple hours later Percival woke to a new supply of food and water in the chest. He ate and drank gratefully and then went to find Barwick. The boatman had said he wanted to talk and Percival was curious as to what he wanted. He also wanted to find out how close they were to the voyage's end.

Barwick was standing on the deck, in the same spot that he stood during their other conversation.

"You're here again," Barwick said.

"What is it you wanted to talk to me about?"

Barwick turned to look out over the water. He shrugged and pulled his cloak tighter about him. The sky was a bright green today and there were no clouds. The wind was not nearly as strong as it had been and the water seemed to be calmer.

"There are less spirits on this part of the River," Barwick said explaining the peaceful calm.

"I'm glad to hear it," Percival replied.

"You met Norhan, did you?" Barwick asked.

"Yes," Percival said. "I did not know he had died. He's a strange fellow."

"That he is," Barwick said with a smile. "He's what I wanted to talk to you about."

"Really?" Percival asked suspiciously.

"Norhan is very valuable to the overlord. My spies have told me that there is an effort underway to intercept him. I need to avoid that at all costs."

"And what does that have to do with me?"

"I would like you to escort the prophet to my people. I will equip you with a sword and it will be your mission to see that he is safely turned over to one of my lieutenants."

"Absolutely not," Percival said.

Barwick looked Percival in the eye. His face was stern yet

desperate. He seemed to be a man down to his last option.

"I cannot tell you how important all of this is," Barwick said. "Norhan must be dropped off at the city, Riverbank. My people are in that city and they will take him off of your hands. Besides, I was told that you would help me."

"Told by who?" Percival asked. "Who would have told you that I would protect Norhan?"

"Your former warlord," Barwick said.

Percival's eyes bulged in surprise. Caltrin. Caltrin! The magician was fighting alongside Barwick. For a moment, Percival wanted to accept the task. It would mean getting to see Caltrin once again. And how he wanted to see the man he loved like a father. How he wanted to embrace his former lord.

"No," Percival said again. "I left this life behind me when I died."

"You left nothing behind Percival," Barwick said. "I know your fate and I know you know your fate. Norhan told you what it was to be last night and you pretend not to know."

"Fate can be changed," Percival said.

"Only when it wants to be," Barwick replied.

"I don't want to get involved in this war," Percival said. "I am weary of war."

"Escort him," Barwick said again. "If you do this, we will hide you elsewhere in the world, far away from the fighting where you can live in peace."

"Really?" Percival asked.

"I swear it," Barwick said. "But know this. Your fate is absolute. You will fight. You will be forced to fight. The final wars are underway and when the time comes, I will welcome you into my service."

"Believe me," Barwick said. "I would rather go about this in a different way. I could drop him off at our main outpost in the Savage Land where he will be safe from Serpintus but he is demanding to go to Riverbank."

"Why do you have to do what he wants?" Percival asked.

"Norhan has to go to Riverbank. I do not know why exactly but he says that he will not receive his vision unless everything happens the way he has foreseen."

"This is the most ridiculous thing I have ever heard," Percival said.

"That it is, but it is very important that we listen to him. He is going to tell me how to end the war."

"In my experience you either win, lose or compromise."

"No," Barwick said. "He will tell me what I need to know to destroy the minions."

Percival spent the rest of the day regretting this conversation. Indeed, he was so distracted by what Barwick had asked of him that he had forgotten to ask how long until they reached the shore. He was not sure he wanted to reach the shore now. Barwick vanished after the conversation and Percival could not find him.

Back in his cabin Percival found that the chest that before had been filled with food and a skin of water had grown in length. He opened the chest and saw a shield and a sword lying on top of more clothing. There was a green tunic with black pants and brown boots. The shield was round and had no symbol. The sword was in a black scabbard. The hilt was brown and the blade itself was so bright that Percival saw his eyes reflected in it. There was something else in the chest, pinned to the underside of the lid. It was a note.

Walk through Riverbank.
My man, Wulfric will find you.
He will guide you to safety.
Protect the prophet.

Percival read the note twice and nodded. He donned the

clothing, strapped the sword belt over his shoulder and slung the shield onto his back. Now that there was a sword at his side, the feeling of naked vulnerability left him. How strange it was that a weapon could make him feel that much safer.

¤

Riverbank.

He was curious about this place since it was where he was going to be dropped off. The feeling of nervousness crept into his stomach again. Here it was, the afterlife. The thing that was, for the living, both a fear and a consolation.

Percival walked onto the deck as the ship approached the docks of a massive city. Percival's breath was taken away at the first sight of it. There were towering structures of brick and stone that stretched into the emerald sky. He had never seen buildings that size. Armora was filled with wood and thatch halls with earth floors. These buildings looked greater than the all of the royal palaces and stronger even than most of the forts that dotted the borders of the kingdom.

"I've never," he said to himself as he marveled at the size of the structures.

"That is Riverbank," a voice said behind Percival. The former warlord turned and saw that Norhan had come to join him on the deck. "I knew this place years before I actually died."

"It is marvelous," Percival said.

"It's dangerous," Norhan said. "I have seen it so much lately that I fear it."

"What is there to fear?"

"This place, the Otherworld, is a place to fear. There is no law and no government. The minions dominate it and Serpintus rules the minions. He doesn't care about humanity though. We will see much evil in our time at Riverbank alone. We will see horrors throughout the rest of the Otherworld.

"No law," Percival said. "Barwick said that he has people stationed there. I'm supposed to take you to them."

"Yes, indeed," Norhan said. "I have foreseen this very conversation. We will begin my Great Charade."

Norhan turned to walk back to his cabin and when Percival called after him to ask what he had meant; Norhan simply waved a hand to indicate that he was not going to talk about it.

Chapter Three

Barwick's true allegiance has been brought into question a number of times, but there is something in his dark past which propels him to ferry the dead and lead the resistance against the minions. Few know what caused Barwick's initial rebellion and few know the pain that drives the boatman.

Percival and Norhan walked through the streets of Riverbank cautiously. Norhan too had been equipped with a sword and shield though the prophet himself had declared that he had never used a sword and that he never would.

Percival found Norhan's company irritating. He wanted to be rid of him and he wanted to see Caltrin. That was the real reason he had taken this mission. Caltrin had suggested him and therefore it was Caltrin who asked. He had a hard time turning down his former lord.

The people of Riverbank seemed content to keep to themselves. Percival was glad of this. The buildings may have been magnificent but the people were all unwashed peasants who looked like they'd rob you as soon as speak to you.

Where was Wulfric?

Percival began feeling worried about the situation the closer it came to nightfall. He had thought that Wulfric would have taken Norhan off his hands within half an hour and that had not happened. Hours had passed since the dead walked in a single file off of the boat and still there was no sign of Wulfric.

"Maybe he was mugged and killed and Barwick didn't know," Percival thought.

Darkness began sweeping over the city and Percival and Norhan were still walking. It was a large city, larger than any Percival had seen in his life. He figured he would have cleared it by nightfall but now it still stretched on miles ahead.

"I'm tired," Norhan said.

"Me too," Percival said. "But we have nowhere to stop."

Norhan turned down a side street and Percival followed.

"What are you doing?" Percival asked.

"The next thing I'm supposed to do," Norhan replied. "There are two people down here who are going to help us. Do not worry. We shall meet Wulfric soon and you will be rid of me."

"That will be a relief," Percival said. "How soon?"

"In a few hours."

Percival and Norhan walked down the side street which seemed to be three miles long. Finally Norhan stopped at a house. It was a curiously small house between the buildings. It was only one story and made of wood. It was the closest resemblance to the homes of the people of Armora that Percival had so far seen. Norhan rapped on the door three times and then waited.

The door swung open and a young girl stood in its frame. She was small, and had red hair that was a tangled mess that she held back with a black string. She had a calculating look in her eyes as if she were analyzing everything that she saw. The two strangers on her doorstep caused her apprehension and that showed on her face which tightened when she saw the swords the men were carrying.

"Your name is Heleina," Norhan said.

"Who are you?" she asked.

"Friends," Norhan replied.

"Really? That's hard to believe."

"Is your brother here?" Norhan asked.

It seemed that what he knew about Heleina was catching her off guard. For a time she looked as if she was trying to recognize Percival and Norhan from a time in the past but she soon realized that she had never met either of them and so tightened her face once again.

"We are newly arrived in the Otherworld," Norhan said. "We were hoping to stay in your house for the night."

"Heleina?" a male voice asked from inside the house. "Who is at the door?"

"Strangers with swords," Heleina said.

A young man appeared in the doorway behind Heleina and looked at Percival and Norhan with nervousness.

"Listen," the boy said, "we don't have any gold so please don't hurt us. We have nothing."

"Julron," Norhan said, "we do not want your money, just your time."

"Who are you?" Julron echoed Heleina's earlier question.

"Might we come inside? Then we can talk?" Norhan asked.

Heleina and Julron exchanged worried looks. Norhan sighed.

"If we take off our weapons," Norhan said, "might we be able to speak with you both?"

Julron and Heleina nodded reluctantly.

"It's okay, Percival," Norhan said. "I've seen this before. We will be safe."

Percival didn't want to trust Norhan's judgment on this but decided to do so anyway. This was not the land of reason but the land of magic and Gods. He unhooked the scabbard from his belt and handed it and the sword to Heleina while Norhan did the same and handed his to Julron.

"Now may we come in, friends?" Norhan asked.

"You may," Heleina said.

Percival and Norhan entered the house which was sparsely furnished. There was a small wooden table in the middle of the large room and several wooden chairs. There were two cots set up as beds for Julron and Heleina with thin blankets. Against the wall was a barrel filled with water and beside the barrel was two buckets apparently used to gather water to refill the barrel. It was simple, like the peasant homes in Cadan Mol. Percival felt more at home than before by just being in this one room house.

Julron and Heleina each held a sword as they offered their unannounced guests seats. Percival saw the distrust in their eyes but thought nothing of it. The common people were always afraid of those carrying weapons. Why should the Otherworld's common people be any different?

"So you guys just died?" Julron asked trying to break the silence.

"We just arrived today," Percival said. "How long have you two been dead?"

"Just over a year," Julron replied. "Been here in Riverbank for most of that time."

Norhan stared fixedly at Heleina and did not remove his gaze when she saw him staring. Julron and Percival noticed it too. Percival was used to Norhan's strange behavior by now but Julron and Heleina were puzzled.

"What?" Heleina asked.

"Fate is intertwined," Norhan said.

"What?" Julron asked.

"I said that fate is intertwined. You are both about to go through hardship but you will come out of it in greater positions. There will be death though and you both will cause it."

"Crazy man," Julron said.

Julron and Heleina drew the swords from their scabbards and brandished them menacingly. "Stay back!" Heleina yelled.

"What are you doing?" Norhan asked. He knew the answer already.

"You're crazy," Heleina said. "We have dealt with crazy people here already. I will kill you if you move."

"Fine," Norhan said. Percival was thinking of a way to overpower the boy and so retrieve a sword.

"Now, who are you?" Heleina asked.

"I am called Norhan."

"And how did you know us?"

"You told me all about you and your brother," Norhan said, "months from now."

"What?"

"I am a prophet," Norhan explained. "Perhaps you have heard of me. I am on the run from Serpintus, as it were. This man here," Norhan gestured at Percival, "is my escort until I can meet up with Barwick's people."

"Really?" Heleina asked skeptically.

"It is the truth," Norhan said. "Would you like me to prove I am a prophet?"

"Yes," Heleina said.

"Very well. What do you want me to predict?"

Heleina thought about this for a moment. It would have to be something difficult, something that couldn't easily be explained away.

"Do you know my ambition?" she asked Norhan. "It is the one thing I vowed crossing the river. Only Julron knows it. Do I confide this to you?"

"About turning your father into a ghost after he dies? Yes. You were supposed to tell me this in a month."

Heleina narrowed her eyes. She had spoken truthfully. Never had she breathed a word of this desire to anyone else and yet this man knew it.

"And will I succeed?" Heleina asked. "If you can see the future, you obviously know."

Norhan hesitated to answer. He thought of telling a lie but then thought better of it. The truth was that he didn't know. He couldn't know. There was a time in the near future where his powers would go away. And though he looked as far ahead as his sight would let him, he could not see Heleina and Julron killing their father. He decided that truth was best at the moment.

"I can't see that far ahead," Norhan said.

"Of course not," Heleina said.

"But if you give me your hand, I can look into your future further than I can see into my own."

Heleina hesitated again but then shrugged. "Watch him, Julron," she said. She then lowered the sword and held a hand out for Norhan.

Norhan grasped the hand and his blue eyes suddenly turned white. This was no mere glimpse of the future for him. He was peering years ahead. His mind was filled with images of Heleina's future. He saw as far as he possibly could and then pulled back. He did not tell Heleina what he had seen for it was too horrible. She did not ask what all he had seen. She just wanted to know if she succeeded.

"No," Norhan said truthfully. "I did not see you succeed."

Heleina nodded and then assured him that she would like to believe in the possibility and not take a prophecy to heart. Norhan nodded and seemed amused. People were so ready to believe good fortunes but rejected the dark ones.

"Our minds are now connected," Norhan told her in a tone that expressed a warning. "Remember that."

Gradually Julron and Heleina began to let go of their uneasiness with Percival and Norhan.

"Have you seen anyone that you knew in life?" Percival asked.

"You mean old friends and family who died before us?" Julron asked, and then shook his head. "We've looked for a little bit. But then we were running. It's a big place, the Otherworld."

"Yes it is," Percival said. "I was hoping to see my friends again but the enormity of this place makes me think I may spend an eternity searching but never find them."

Moonlight bathed the street outside. Percival noticed how bright everything looked first and then he saw a person walk past the house. Another soon followed. And then another.

"What's going on?" Percival asked. It seemed late for anyone to be wandering the streets.

"The garden is opening," Heleina explained.

"The garden?"

"It's our source of food," Heleina said. "It opens around midnight. The trees come alive and provide fruit. Of course, you have to pay to use it. One gold coin and you can eat."

Percival realized that he was truly hungry. He guessed Norhan would be too.

"Are you planning on going to this garden?" he asked.

"I think we need to, Heleina," Julron said from across the room. He had opened a floorboard and was pointing at it. "We are out."

"Okay," Heleina said. "We'll have to go." She then addressed Percival and Norhan. "Are either of you hungry?"

"Very much so," Percival said.

"And you have no gold?" she asked.

"None, I'm afraid."

"It's fine. We can cover you. Come with us."

Heleina and Julron led them through the city. Percival had requested his sword back and they had given it back without argument. They also tried to give Norhan's back but Norhan said that Julron was better suited for the weapon. The boy now walked with the blade sheathed at his side.

Down the side street they went, all three miles of it. Then Heleina and Julron turned onto the main road that Percival and Norhan had been travelling down earlier that day. They remained on that road for a time, walking in the opposite direction than Percival and Norhan had come.

They turned a corner and walked down another side street. They turned from that side street onto another and their path wound between the buildings like a maze. It was clear that Julron and Heleina had done this many times for neither of them seemed to even think about which direction to take. It was second nature.

"There it is," Julron said.

At the end of the short side street was an enclosed place with walls as tall as the buildings surrounding them. There was a line of people but the line was moving swiftly. As the four came closer to the entrance, Percival saw that everyone had to drop a gold coin into a cylinder that was attached to the right side of the iron gate. Once the gold was received the gate would swing open only to close once again after the person who had deposited the coin had gone through.

Julron handed a coin to Norhan and Percival as they approached the gate. When it was their turn, they each dropped their coin into the cylinder. The coins vanished and then the gate swung open. Once they had walked through the gate slammed shut behind them.

"How do we get back out?" Percival asked Norhan.

Norhan shrugged.

Julron and Heleina came through next and then the four walked into the lush green area of the garden. Percival could see the garden's bounty from a distance. The gate they had gone through had led into a long hallway of sorts with towering stone walls on either side. There were torches lining each wall to light the way, though the moon was so bright that the torchlight seemed redundant.

There was a line of people waiting to get through the final entrance and into the garden. It was there that people could scatter and move about the large open space and pick what food they wanted. It seemed a good amount of people were content with examining the trees at the very end of the stone hall. This had caused a backup that made the people who had not yet reached the garden impatient.

"Every time," Julron said.

Someone near the front of the line had become impatient and began shoving people out of his way. This was a bald man with a large frame. Of course, someone challenged this man as he pushed his way through and one fool actually put a hand on the man's shoulder to pull him back. This person received a fist in his jaw. Another person, standing next to the man who had been punched, lunged at the big man and tackled him to the ground. The big man turned his new attacker over and struck him once, leaving him unconscious. Then there was the press of people trying to move further ahead in the line. These people surrounded the big man who let out a cry of outrage and kicked a random person in the groin. A full fight erupted as people came to the aid of their friends who were being struck down and more people who were unintentionally hit began fighting back.

"Bastards!" the big man yelled. He seemed to be able to hold his own and managed to stand and fight an assault from all sides.

"Come on," Julron said. He and Heleina guided Percival and Norhan through the uproar of people. It was something they were accustomed to.

"No civilization in the Otherworld," Heleina said when they were clear of the brawling crowd.

"There was no civilization in the mortal world," Percival said sadly. "Why should there be civilization here?"

¤

The garden was massive but was also packed with people. There were walkways that wound around trees and vines and shrubs. At one end of the garden there were rows of tables. Fountains dotted the area of the garden. In the center, curiously enough, was a tavern.

Julron and Heleina opened knapsacks that they had carried beneath their cloaks and began dropping food into them. Each thing that was picked grew back in a matter of seconds. Percival and Norhan filled their stomachs on the fruit of the trees.

When the four had eaten their fill and the knapsacks were full, Percival wanted to go to the tavern.

"They have mead in the Otherworld?" he asked.

"Better mead than any in the mortal world," Heleina said. "But it costs more gold to drink than it does to eat."

They contented themselves by drinking the water from one of the fountains. That, at least, did not cost more gold. They sat on stone benches and looked across the garden bathed in moonlight. The enclosed walls gave a sense of being in a fortress and Percival had an image of archers posted on the wall flash briefly through his mind.

"Are all the gardens like this?" Percival asked.

"Don't know," Julron said. "This is the only one that we've been to. They're supposed to be all over the place."

Each of them had wooden cups that they filled with water from the fountain. The water was remarkable in its cleanliness but none of them seemed to notice. They washed down the aftertaste of the fruit and vegetables in silence.

As they sat and drank they did not notice a man staring at them. He was a tall man with long black hair that hung down his back in plaits. He had no facial hair of any kind and his eyes were a dark blue. He had on a red cloak that covered his entire body.

"You are newly dead," the man said from where he was standing.

Percival turned and saw the man had been talking to them. "Yes," Percival said.

"Unfortunate for you then."

"Why?" Percival asked.

"This is a hell. The people suffer and live short afterlives. You'll be spending most of your time in hiding, I think. These people here are lucky enough to escape the overlord's notice but if he gets angry or bored, he'll kill. And you don't want to be around when he decides to kill."

Percival looked about the vicinity of the fountain. He noticed people staring but they turned away as he caught their glance. "Just who might you be?" he asked the man.

"My name is Wulfric," the man said.

"Finally!" Percival exclaimed. "I was supposed to meet up with you. You're to take Norhan off my hands."

"You make it sound like I'm such fine company," Norhan said drily

"Lord Barwick told me to find you two and escort you," Wulfric said.

Percival regarded Wulfric for a moment. He was not the sort of man he had expected. Wulfric seemed vain about his looks, his carefully plaited hair and clean, bright red cloak reminded Percival of a bard that had entertained Cadan Mol years ago. Everyone else in the garden wore tattered rags but the cloak Wulfric wore seemed to reflect the moonlight, and there was no hole on it anywhere.

"You are Former Lord Percival?" Barwick asked.

"Yes," Percival said. "I am Former Lord Percival." He despised calling himself that. "Where will you be taking us, Lord Wulfric?"

"It's just Wulfric. I am no lord. I'll be taking you to our

underground hideout in the center of Riverbank. I am told that Norhan is very valuable to the overlord."

Wulfric scratched at his chin and then suddenly made a sharp turn of his head. The sound of a sudden gasp had drawn his attention and across the garden he saw the cause of the gasp. Two men, soldiers by the looks of them, had removed their peasant cloaks and revealed the armor they wore underneath. These two men also drew their swords.

"We need to get out of here," he said. "Now."

Percival saw the soldiers and asked Wulfric why they would be here. The soldiers had seen Wulfric and had watched as he made contact with the four. They had assumed one of the four was the prophet that Serpintus wanted and so they had sprung into action.

"They are of the overlord," Wulfric explained.

"And what do they want?" Julron asked.

Wulfric pointed at Norhan. "Him," he said. "Follow me, and for the Gods' sake, do exactly as I tell you.

Wulfric tried to lead them into a crowd of people but luck was not on his side. The soldiers closed in on the crowd and brandished their blades at the mass of people, growling insults and threats as they did it. The people moved out of their way and left Wulfric and his four followers exposed.

"Run!" Wulfric yelled.

Percival and company were running through the garden. Percival's earlier question about how to leave the garden was answered as Wulfric led them through a hall similar to the entrance. The difference was that the gate at the end of this hall was all too willing to open without coins and even more eager to close in the wake of those departed.

The soldiers were closing in on them fast so Wulfric had to act. There was a line of people still headed to the garden that the five crossed. When they did, Wulfric toppled two people over who then inadvertently tripped the soldiers.

Wulfric then led the four down an alleyway and halfway down he stopped and turned down an alley within the alley. Once they were all in this very narrow space Wulfric motioned for them to stay low and be quiet.

"What are you doing?" Percival hissed.

Wulfric said nothing but sure enough, a few minutes later, the armed men ran past them, and down the street. They still believed that the five were shifting their way through the seemingly never-ending maze of alleys.

"We're safe for now," Wulfric said.

Julron plucked Wulfric's shoulder. "Why are they after Norhan?"

It was Norhan himself who replied. "I am dangerous to Serpintus. I know things, or rather, I will know things that he wants to know and doesn't want Barwick knowing. He'll try to get the truth out of me or he will kill me before I can tell one of Barwick's people."

"He'll kill you?" Percival asked. "How can you know that already?"

"I am a prophet, Percival," Norhan said with an exasperated voice.

Chapter Four

The absence of the Gods allowed the evil to dwell among the good. All came to the Otherworld, whether righteous holy men or cruel murderers. Left to the minions, the Otherworld became more and more like the mortal world until only superficial differences remained.

Wulfric successfully led the four fugitives to a rundown house in the slums of Riverbank. Hours had passed since they escaped the soldiers and they were finally allowed to move from their hiding place. The slum was a short walk from where they had been hiding. It was not a slum compared to mortal world standards. Most forts and palaces that took years to construct paled in comparison to the poor buildings of Riverbank. Yet, according to Wulfric, all of Riverbank was the slum of the Otherworld. Wulfric had no patience for the questions Heleina and Julron asked and Percival knew most of the information already so he did not add his voice to their queries. Norhan began to answer some of them however. It seemed that Serpintus was afraid because Norhan was the first prophet to come across the River of Souls since the time of the Gods. It is said that there will be three prophets who come before the final wars. The three prophets will be the end of Serpintus.

Inside an old building, which was built of brick and stone, Wulfric led them down a flight of stairs. There was a circular door at the bottom. Wulfric pulled a whistle from his pockets and blew into it three times, each time a different pitch. The door opened. It did not swing open like the gate at the garden but creaked open slowly. Beyond the door was a dark tunnel.

"Not to worry," Wulfric said. He looked around the room and found an unlit torch. He gestured for the four to follow him. When he stepped into the tunnel, the torch erupted into green flames before receding to normal size and turning orange.

"What is this place? Percival asked.

"This is a tunnel that leads to every section of the city," Wulfric replied. "We will go a little ways. Our hideout is not far from here."

As they walked, Percival asked what the tunnels were and Wulfric replied that ages ago they were built for the transportation of the overlord's soldiers. They could march from one end of the city to the other without being seen. He needed this, Wulfric explained, because Riverbank was his capital after the Gods left. Only after he had conquered all he could conquer did he abandon the city and the tunnels. But the tunnels lasted until a great earthquake shook the city. The earthquake, ironically enough, had been caused by Serpintus as a punishment for Riverbank. It left the tunnels sealed. They remained that way for centuries until the new rebellion started. Caltrin, the magician, had cleared them with his magic and had sealed them against any of the minions. Only those in the rebellion could gain access. The torches were Caltrin's magic as well.

After a short walk through several turns, the five were finally standing before another circular door. Wulfric played the same three notes on his whistle and the door creaked open.

"This is our Riverbank hideout," Wulfric said, "or as we like to call it, the Sanctuary."

The Sanctuary was large enough to house a great crowd of people but there were only a dozen people there when the five entered. Wulfric led the fugitives to a hooded man who had stood when he saw the door open.

"Lord Palcron," Wulfric said, bowing his head.

"Wulfric," Palcron said.

"I have found the prophet and the protector. The other two were with them. They are in danger."

"Thank you, Wulfric," Palcron said.

"Wait here," Wulfric said to the four.

He vanished into the shadows and was gone for a few minutes. When he returned he was flanked by two men, each with swords clasped at their sides.

"This is Grulan and Narock," he said. He turned to either side and addressed the two men. "This is Percival, Julron, Heleina and Norhan."

Grulan had short black hair and a red scar across his face. He stood a head taller than Wulfric and was dressed entirely in black. The sword at his side looked heavier than the one Wulfric used. Narock had a long beard tied at his chest. His sword looked lighter than Grulan's and he too was dressed in black. Percival thought that either of these men looked like brutes that he would have comfortable standing shoulder to shoulder with in a shield-wall.

"They are going to be your guard should you need to go to the surface for any reason. You will take them with you."

Percival reluctantly agreed. He was not used to strangers having any authority over him. In many ways he felt more inadequate and insignificant than he had the first time he had wielded a spear among seasoned warriors.

They settled in to the Sanctuary easy enough. Percival found a mirror and a sharp knife and shaved off his newly grown beard and then cut his hair. The reflection in the mirror was Percival as a young man.

Wulfric tried to make them comfortable and Palcron promised that he would speak to them when he had a chance. Wulfric showed them a room filled with cots where they could sleep. "There're more rooms like this down here. We can house an army."

Julron and Heleina had been shaken by their recent experiences. They had avoided the minions for so long but now they were hiding underground. And all of this was for helping a couple of strangers.

It had been something that they had talked about secretly. They knew that they hated the minions and had seen firsthand some of the horrible things the minions had done. It all seemed far too impossible to dream of standing against it. It seemed a task for more worthy people. Even the people's champion, Caltrin, didn't seem to be strong enough to make a difference.

"Are you liking this?" Heleina asked Julron when they were finally alone.

"Why would I have an opinion?" Julron asked. "I have no right to like anything in the Otherworld. None of us do."

"I don't need a philosophy lesson," Heleina said. "Are you ready to be in a rebellion?"

Julron thought about this for a while. He and Heleina had died fairly young but Julron had always imagined himself a warrior. He loved the thought of being a hero of the people on the countryside, of riding into battle beneath his own banner. He had never fought in a battle, however. He had trained for them. But his coming of age happened during a time of peace, a time in which few battle-hardened warriors did any kind of combat. It was at such a time that he and Heleina died. Dead before he could achieve his dream. Dead by toadstools in his mushroom stew. Murder by a loathsome man who dared call himself Father.

"There will be no wealth as a rebel," Julron said.

"None," Heleina agreed.

"That could only come by joining Serpintus' army."

"Which is not acceptable." And Heleina did more than state that fact. The tone in her voice ordered Julron to avoid considering the side of the minions.

Julron was considering though. He had been considering for a long time. The minions had total control. They were like gods in a way and it was a fool's game to attempt to stand up to them no matter how evil they were. His conscience couldn't let him take the steps his logical mind commanded. He would rather have honor than wealth.

"You should sleep, Percival," Norhan said. It was night and the people in the Sanctuary had gone to bed. All except for those on guard duty, that is. Percival had been lying in the dark not making a sound and Norhan had had his back turned to him. Yet Norhan knew he was awake. "Of course it's no use telling you to sleep. You and I are about to have a conversation."

"How can you see the future like that?" Percival asked.

Norhan shrugged. "I have been able to since I was a child. I remember the first thing I saw was a vision of a raid that killed my father. I saw him die. I tried to warn him but he didn't listen to me. He just said that it was a foolish dream and that I should focus on my chores and helping my mother. He was a farmer, you see? He said he couldn't pack up everything and leave. We needed food, he told me. And we need some income. I told him that food and income were worthless to a dead man and he struck me. That night, enemy riders came, burned the town, stole what they could and set fire to the fields. My father was cut down before my eyes in the exact way I had seen in my dream.

"My mother had known about my prophecy of my father's death and she had shrugged it off like my father had. Now she tried to test it. She would frequently ask questions about things that were about to happen. At first she would ask about the upcoming harvest or about the birth of a child in the village. Then she started asking things like whether rain would come or if our animals would be safe for the night if we did not pen them in.

"Eventually she saw my ability as a way of income. She began charging other villagers a gold piece and in return I would answer something about the villager's future.

"I was always accurate," Norhan said sadly. "Do you know how awful it is to know everything that will happen before it happens? To have your dreams bombarded by images of every possible future? To see something happen and know not only what will happen but what could have happened if a different action had been taken? It's hell!"

Percival looked at Norhan with pity. This was a man not unlike himself. Percival had been forced into being a soldier while Norhan had been forced into being a prophet. Neither of them were fond of the gifts they had. He wondered what Norhan would do if he didn't have the powers of prophecy.

"I was wondering," Percival said. "You said that Fate has plans of me. That I was what I am and not what I want to be. What did you mean by that?"

"It means that you want to avoid being a soldier, but you can't. You were a great warrior in life, Percival, but soon you'll become one of the greatest in existence."

"No," Percival said softly but definitely.

"I have seen it," Norhan said. "You are going to be a hero of the Otherworld."

"About that," Percival said, "what is it you need to tell Barwick?"

"I don't know."

"But you can see the future."

"It's a vision that has not been revealed to me. Only if things happen the exact way they are supposed to happen will the vision be revealed."

"So you have no idea then?"

"I know what I need to do. I know when it will be revealed to me. I know that what will be revealed is probably the way to kill the minions and end the hell of the Otherworld."

Sleep at last came for Percival. It was deep and dreamless while Norhan's was plagued by the future. Nothing was shocking for Norhan. He had even known how the Otherworld would be before he crossed the River of Souls. He had known he would meet Lord Percival before he had succumbed to the disease which ended his life. He had even known that he would be a fugitive from the overlord and hidden underground. And now he dreamed of what would come next.

¤

In the Sanctuary there was a library. It contained many pieces of information on the history of the Otherworld as well as some things on the history of the mortal world. Percival was nearly overwhelmed when he saw the scroll-filled shelves lining the walls of one of the side rooms.

"It's amazing," Percival said.

"Knowledge is something that the dead value," Grulan said in explanation. Grulan had shown this to Percival after a conversation the two had had that morning. Percival had revealed that he had always wanted to be a scholar and Grulan decided he would want to see the library.

"It is not much really compared to other libraries in the world," Grulan said. "Lord Palcron keeps this one in order and encourages anyone in his alliance to donate to it. Did you do much studying in life?"

"More than normal, I would say." Percival ran his hands along the shelves. "I was never a scholar because I was too busy being a warrior but I would try to study writings every chance I got."

There was a table and a bench at the end of the room. On that table was a candle. There was really no need for the candle as the library was filled with the magical light that filled the Sanctuary – Caltrin's light.

"I'll leave you to it," Grulan said.

"Thank you," Percival replied. "Really."

When Grulan was gone Percival began looking through the scrolls. He found history that told of the rise of the overlord. Sitting down at the table, he unfastened the clasp and unrolled the scroll. He began to read the history of the post-god Otherworld. This was not what he read, word-for-word, but rather an overview of what had happened in the Otherworld up until the point in which he crossed over.

¤

Ages ago, the Gods lived among humanity's dead souls. The Otherworld was created as a place for the dead to exist peacefully, a second life. Before this, the souls of the dead were ghosts plaguing the living but the Otherworld had changed that. There was no true immortality in the Otherworld, however. Though aging was an impossibility, it was still possible to die in an accident of some sort or to be murdered. If a soul died in the Otherworld, that soul would be trapped in the River of Souls where it would remain for eternity.

Mankind lived happily enough and the Gods, known as the Triad of Light, were mostly benevolent. There were those Gods however who were not benevolent. Those Gods of Darkness hated the Gods of the Otherworld and so conspired to turn their creation on Them. They came to the Otherworld where They converted followers. Soon the Gods of Light and the Gods of Darkness were at war with humanity divided and lines drawn. Wreckage and devastation consumed the Otherworld and it was then that the Gods of Darkness created a race of beings similar to the angels of the Triad of Light.. They would be referred to as the Dark Gods' minions and the name stuck. Even after years of dominance in the Otherworld they were still called the minions. The Gods of Darkness returned to Their own realm and left the minions behind.

Humanity was weary of war and believed that their Gods were the cause of it. Unanimously they turned on the Gods and sided with the minions. It was true that the Gods could have struck down the minions and commanded the respect and worship of Their creation but at that moment they did not do that. They wanted respect from Their creation for creating them, not for scaring them into obedience. They were hurt. They knew also that the minions were evil and would rise to power in Their absence. The Gods, nevertheless, disappeared. Humanity was left in the hands of the minions.

The minions did not fight amongst themselves for control of the humans. The greatest of the minions, Serpintus, rallied them together and began beating the humans into submission. A peaceful theocracy was turned into a cruel and brutal dictatorship. Everything fell to a state of hell.

Many have tried to overthrow the minions but there is a massive army that protects the rulers of the Otherworld. And even if that army is defeated, it is no small thing to kill a minion. They are nearly indestructible. To fight one means almost guaranteed defeat.

With each failed rebellion, Serpintus has grown more efficient in dealing with his enemies. Most resistance is forced into the Savage Land where the empire of Serpintus does not reach, where wild demons live. When rebel movements retreat to the Savage Land, they are never heard from again.

¤

Percival rolled up the scroll and placed it back on the shelf. He sat in silence for a long time, thinking over what he had read. He wondered if it was all true. He had been told that the Gods were silent in the mortal world because They were busy in the Otherworld but now he learned They were not even here anymore. He knew he was in a rebellion now. His involvement had been purely circumstantial, but he was here.

The door opened and woke Percival from his thoughts. Norhan had entered and was walking to the table.

"Not a great story is it?" Norhan said. "The overlord being a creation of evil Gods."

"No," Percival said.

"His reign will end soon. Don't worry."

"And the Gods will return?"

Norhan closed his eyes for a moment and opened them again. "I do not know. But his reign will end."

"But you said he will kill you. If he kills you, how can you know that his reign will end?"

"I can hear the whispers of Fate," Norhan said. "I feel that it will end and I do believe that I am correct."

Chapter Five

It is thought that Serpintus has a hatred for humanity but this is not entirely true. Serpintus and all of the minions are specially conditioned to regard humans as animals to be dominated. This was implanted into their minds by their Creators and has remained there ever since. Only one has broken the conditioning to help the humans... Barwick.

The Lord of Riverbank, Tragor, sat worrying about the message he had just received. It had been a week since the prophet had escaped his men and then disappeared and now he was about to be punished for his incompetence. The message had come as a dust figure of the man sending it. The dust figure told Tragor to expect the overlord by the day's end. Tragor listened with disbelief. There was a feeling of deep fear gripping his heart.

There would be no explanation that Serpintus might accept, Tragor feared. The overlord was not one to show mercy when dealing with an incompetent lord. The fact that he was handling this himself was evidence that he wanted to make Tragor suffer.

Tragor was interrupted from his dark daydreams by the beginning of their manifestation. Serpintus had arrived. He had no entourage with him. He had not come in a carriage nor on horseback. He had flown.

Flying was a power that only the overlord possessed. There were rumors that the magician, Caltrin could also fly but Tragor had never seen the man do it. Serpintus had a deep control over the magic of the Otherworld and he could use it for his own purposes. Serpintus landed on the doorstep to Tragor's mansion. He had a hand on the hilt of the saber that he kept at his side and wore a look of contempt on his pale face. He pushed his way past Tragor when he had opened mansion door.

"My lord," Tragor said bowing his head.

"If I were you Tragor, I would kneel," Serpintus growled.

Tragor obeyed and knelt, facing Serpintus. The door was still open.

"Stand up!" Serpintus said irritably. The overlord was wearing a black cloak over a jewel-embroidered suit of grey and black. He had pale skin on his face which was in contrast to his black spiky hair. There were grey gloves over his hands. One hand remained fastened to the hilt of the sword.

"Are you going to close the door?" Serpintus asked.

"I am, my lord," Tragor said humbly. He hurried to close the door while Serpintus waited.

"I think you know why I'm here," Serpintus said.

"Yes Lord," Tragor said. "I am sorry about losing the prophet."

"And how exactly did that happen?" Serpintus asked.

"My men lost him by the garden. He had help from some other people. I think Barwick told him how to evade us."

"Correct me if I am wrong," Serpintus said. "I warned you about this when you were in my court last did I not?"

"You did, lord," Tragor said.

"So how many men did you send to apprehend him?" Serpintus asked.

"I sent a dozen into the city. Six pairs. Only one pair saw the him however."

"And now our enemy has the prophet," Serpintus said. "Did it occur to you to send more men? To wait near all the drop off points? To do everything in you power to make sure that I got the prophet?"

"Forgive me, Lord," Tragor said.

"How dare you demand anything of me!" Serpintus roared.

Tragor looked fearful. The overlord was indeed furious and it seemed that forgiveness was not on his mind. Forgiveness had never been an attribute he had exercised liberally. It was a rare occurrence that Serpintus forgave anything.

"I will not forgive you, simpleton," Serpintus said. "But I will not kill you either."

The relief that showed on Tragor's face was mocked by Serpintus with a sneer. He went on: "I will not kill you but I will make your existence miserable for the foreseeable future."

Tragor did not dare ask how, though he wanted to. Serpintus was ready to unleash wrath at any foolish question Tragor might ask. He waited in silence hoping Serpintus would explain. He wanted to know what to expect, what to deal with.

"The first thing that will happen is the gardens of Riverbank will be dried up. That will put an end to your income."

Tragor was horrified. "For how long?"

"Eternity," Serpintus said.

"No," Tragor said. He saw Serpintus smile at this weak protest and felt that his entire existence was about to crumble. In his despair however there was a small thought in his mind. Serpintus had said that the gardens being dried up was the first thing that would happen. The overlord had more plans. "What else?" Tragor asked.

"I am glad you asked," Serpintus said with a sneer. "I have decided to take decisive action against the rebels that you have let infest this city. I require all of your spearmen."

Serpintus left Tragor's house and walked briskly into the streets of Riverbank. He gripped the hilt of his sword to make himself vanish and move faster. Finally, he came to an old city-square where houses were rundown and boarded up. There was no life in this area except for a man standing on a corner. Serpintus released the grip on the sword and appeared. The man jumped in surprise as the overlord materialized two yards in front of him.

"What do you have for me. Palcron?" Serpintus asked.

"The truth," Palcron replied.

"You have already told me what I need to know. I can raze the city and destroy Caltrin's army. I can get the prophet too."

"There is more," Palcron said. "Caltrin himself is coming to Riverbank."

"Really?" Serpintus' eyes flashed with malevolence.

"He will arrive to meet with Percival, the man who escorted the prophet."

"Then it is then that I will make the declaration of war!" Serpintus said.

"Lord?"

"Caltrin will think to have his people flee instead of fight me. If I threaten to kill every last thing in Riverbank he will not be able to flee. He will put his army and himself between me and the people."

"That does sound like something he would do," Palcron said.

"I thank you for this," Serpintus said. "When the time comes, you will be rewarded for being a good servant. Now go back before you are missed."

¤

Serpintus returned to Tragor's house three hours after he had left and inquired about the spearmen. There were over a hundred men, all well armed. Serpintus voiced his approval and then told Tragor that they would be forming the center of the line of men.

"The center, lord?" Tragor asked.

"I will be storming the city," Serpintus said. "My men are coming from all around and we will gather outside the gates. I want men in the center that know the city."

"Yes, Lord. A wise course of action, Lord."

"Quit your groveling," Serpintus said. "I am sorry that I was so angry earlier. You know that you are one of my few friends and I am not going to kill you."

Tragor breathed a sigh of relief and Serpintus rolled his eyes. The general could be such a simpleton.

"I want to burn the city," Serpintus said. "Perhaps after the battle I will, with my magic. It will show that I am stronger than Caltrin was."

"Indeed, you are."

"During the battle, bring me the prophet."

"Yes. Lord," Tragor said. "He knew that it was likely an impossibility. The prophet would be long gone by the time Serpintus' army arrived. That bastard. Barwick would likely take him away and keep him safe.

Serpintus guessed what Tragor was thinking and said: "I have a man in Riverbank that has good standing with Caltrin and Barwick. He'll deliver the prophet to you."

Serpintus stayed at Tragor's house for the next week. He gathered a portion of his strength there and prepared to invade Riverbank. Messages were sent all over the Otherworld to Serpintus' human followers. A massive amount of spearmen came. It was to be Caltrin's end and that caused excitement among the spearmen. Serpintus decided that once Caltrin was out of the way he would not be complacent like he had been in the past. He had plans to punish the people of the Otherworld. A great devastation would come after this battle.

¤

Percival looked for Wulfric but he was not in the Sanctuary. Palcron told him that Wulfric was frequently travelling the city on errands. He was trusted by Barwick and charged with urgent messages. Percival did learn that his former lord was coming to the Sanctuary. It had seemed like such a long time since Percival had died and one thing kept going through his mind: When am I going to see my friends again? Now he was going to see a friend, an old friend. Caltrin was coming.

There was great anticipation and some apprehension. Caltrin would be the first person Percival had reunited with since his death. What would meeting Caltrin again be like? Would Caltrin think of him as an equal? Indeed Percival had taken over all of Caltrin's positions after the magician's death and he performed his duties without any magic.

Just as he was thinking about Caltrin, wind started to blow. It engulfed the room. Papers flew, pots fell over, Palcron braced himself on a pillar but everyone else fell over. There was a flash of light brighter than the unnatural light that filled the Sanctuary and then something that sounded close to a thunder clap. A man appeared in the middle of the room. He was on one knee with his hands wrapped around a scepter near its globe. The wind died down and the man stood. Percival looked up and made eye contact with his first lord, Caltrin. Percival stepped back in horror as he looked into Caltrin's eyes, or where Caltrin's eyes had been. Instead of eyes, there were two empty sockets filled with green light. Percival got the impression that Caltrin was looking at him and studying his expression.

"I'll tell you all about it in time," Caltrin said.

"Lord Caltrin," Palcron said, letting go of the pillar and stretching an arm for the magician to clasp.

Caltrin flicked his scepter and put the room back to the way it was before his wind had trashed it. Then he turned to Palcron.

"I have troubling news, my friend," Caltrin said.

"More troubling than what has happened recently?" Palcron said. It had been three days since the gardens had dried up and three days since Palcron had met with Serpintus.

"I'll speak with you about it soon."

Percival stepped forward. He was nervous and excited at the same time. "My lord," he said.

Caltrin turned and looked at Percival, his one time second-in-command and his successor. "Percival," he said. "It has been far too long." He pulled Percival into an embrace.

"And it appears I am serving under you again," Percival said.

"From what I hear," Caltrin said after they broke apart, "I may be better off serving you than you serving me. You became a great warrior."

"Not as great as you Lord," Percival said.

"Nonsense," Caltrin said. "You accomplished more than I ever did and you did it without magic. I am honored to fight at you side again."

"I see you still like to make the same entrances," Percival said. "But your scepter was destroyed in your last battle. How did you get a new one?"

"Barwick had it ready for me," Caltrin explained. "I don't know how it got there, but it was waiting for me in my cabin."

"And what happened to your eyes?"

"In time, Percival. In time."

For a time, Caltrin and Percival caught up with one another. Percival relayed an overview of everything that had happened in Armora since Caltrin's death and Caltrin talked about being a protector of the people of Riverbank. It seemed that Caltrin's main occupation was defending the people of the city. Caltrin would not talk about his eyes however and Percival felt curiosity building.

"Lord Caltrin," Palcron said irritably. He had been waiting patiently and was eager to begin.

"Fine, but Percival comes with me," Caltrin said.

Palcron hesitated. It was clear that he did not trust Percival but he also trusted Caltrin's judgment completely. The conflict showed on his face.

"Percival comes with me," Caltrin said once again.

Palcron nodded and then gestured for Percival to follow. The three went to a secluded spot in the sanctuary. Caltrin magically muffled their voices so that only they could hear each other as they spoke and no one else could eavesdrop.

"You have angered the overlord," Caltrin said to Percival.

"Yes, I know."

"He is very angry. There'll be terrible retribution."

"I've heard about the gardens," Percival said.

"But that is not all that Serpintus is doing. He knows that Riverbank is a hotbed for rebel activity and he's ready to crush it once and for all. He's on the warpath."

"He's coming here?" Percival asked.

"Tragor's spearmen are already creating a barrier to keep people in the city. They are being reinforced by the hour by Serpintus' spearmen." Caltrin looked Palcron in the eye as if to suggest the next thing he said was for Palcron only. "I want to fight."

"You cannot be serious," Palcron said.

"Yes, I'm serious," Caltrin replied.

Palcron fought the urge to smile. He was beyond pleased. Caltrin was foolish enough to fight and that meant victory of Serpintus. All the years of fighting were finally coming to an end and Palcron would be rewarded for his secret allegiance to the minions.

"No one can possibly stand against the minions," Palcron said, playing his part. "You may as well be ordering men to kill themselves."

"I order no one to die," Caltrin said. "I will only take volunteers. I will lead the volunteers who are willing to fight and we will meet the overlord's warband. Besides, Serpintus isn't using minions. He is only using his human army."

"Really?"

"Yes. He doesn't think he needs the other minions."

Percival thought of how he had missed this decisive leadership from Caltrin. The magician could look at any situation and see the best outcome and then work toward that outcome no matter how hard it may be to reach it. Something in his voice made Percival feel slightly optimistic. Caltrin always saw further ahead than anyone else.

"Surely the people will turn against us though," Palcron said.

"Naturally," Caltrin seemed unconcerned. "Serpintus has decided to take decisive action and that action is against me. The people are starving and they cannot escape the city to find food elsewhere. I will have a problem rallying them."

"But do you have a plan?" Percival asked.

"I do, old friend," Caltrin gave his former right-hand man a smile. "You see, I want you to take my place as leader of this movement."

There was a stunned silence. Palcron looked indignant and Percival wore an expression of astonishment mixed with repulsion. Had Caltrin really just asked Percival to become leader of a secret army in a war he had no stake in? How could he do that? Anger welled up inside Percival as he thought about how he had been forced into being a warrior by Caltrin when he was young. He had been part of the levy at first and then Caltrin had seen his skill and had invited him to join his warband. Now his life was repeating itself.

"I will not fight," Percival said. "I am done fighting."

Caltrin closed his eyes and sighed in exasperation. "Percival, I need you here."

"No," Percival said. "Listen, I did you a favor by escorting Norhan and I'm ready to leave it all behind."

"I ask you to consider this," Caltrin said. "I know that you didn't want to be a warrior but you were one of the best. If my plan is to work, I would like to know that you are here to lead these people."

Palcron spoke finally. "I am second-in-command!"

"Technically you're not," Caltrin said. "Barwick is the military leader. And Hullsham is the designated ruler if we should win the war. You would be fourth-in-command."

"I should take your place if you plan on dying."

"There," Percival said. "It seems you do not need me after all." Percival stood and walked away from the two men. He shook with anger as he walked. What nerve Caltrin had! But the magician always did have nerve. He always had a way of getting what he wanted. Percival wondered, and not for the first time, whether Caltrin had put a spell over his life, over his existence.

¤

"The Savage Land," Caltrin declared. "The vegetation grows abundant there. Serpintus can't dry it up at all."

"So your plan is to send all of the people to the most dangerous place in the Otherworld?" Palcron asked.

"Yes," Caltrin said. "You see why I didn't want you doing this task."

"It's ludicrous!"

Caltrin suppressed a chuckle. Percival would have been the

ideal choice despite his inexperience in the Otherworld. Palcron was too indecisive to be a good leader. He was good at making sure the rebel forces were organized and equipped but the true leadership was helmed by Caltrin and Barwick. Percival was a natural leader and Barwick had wanted him for the rebel army since they set off across the River.

"That is absurd!" Palcron said.

"How is it absurd?" Caltrin asked.

"I can't lead the people of Riverbank to the Savage Land. We'll be massacred."

"No," Caltrin said. "Serpintus will let you go. He is doing this to get me. Once this battle is over, he will leave you alone for a time."

"Like I said: absurd!"

"Were you an idiot in life?" Caltrin asked.

"What?"

"Do you think that I would suggest something like this if I had no plan for getting the people to safety? Do you?"

"I suppose not," Palcron said reluctantly.

"That's right. You see... I plan for the eventualities. I'm a good leader."

"Will you get on with it then?" Palcron asked.

"The Savage Land will be reached by sea," Caltrin explained. "We have a leader who knows the sea. It will be your task to get the people to the River and loaded onto the ships."

"That doesn't seem like a decent plan," Palcron said. "Can he possibly have enough ships to carry everyone in Riverbank?"

"He will stretch himself to the limit and he will probably leave people behind. I am hoping that I buy enough time to get most to safety. Hopefully if Serpintus kills or captures me, it will be enough for him."

"All of this over a damned prophet," Palcron said.

¤

"Yes," Caltrin agreed. "All of this over a damned prophet."

Percival sat in the library in complete silence. He had a scroll unrolled in front of him but he was not reading it. His eyes scanned over the lines of words but his mind refused to register their meaning. He was still thinking about Caltrin and the audacious demand he had made.

As he was thinking about him, Caltrin entered the library. Percival groaned inwardly and set down the scroll. He looked up at Caltrin with an expression of curiosity. He had wondered how long Caltrin would leave him alone. He also wondered what Caltrin's mood would be like when he finally confronted him. He wasn't afraid of Caltrin's anger but he hoped that the magician would at least be sorry for what he had done. Percival saw from Caltrin's facial expressions that he was sorry.

"You know my feelings about this," Percival said.

"I do," Caltrin agreed. "I never used to believe you though. You said you didn't want to be a man of violence but you were so good at it."

"No one believed me," Percival said. "Especially the kings. Like you said, I was too good. It seemed absurd that I would want to be anything other than a warrior."

Caltrin touched Percival's shoulder and said: "Walk with me."

They walked out of the library and into the Sanctuary. Palcron was nowhere to be seen and there were few people in the Sanctuary. Caltrin led Percival to one of the many doors and into a tunnel.

"These run under the entire city," Caltrin said.

Percival did not respond.

"Since I came here," Caltrin said. "I have fought for Barwick. He has fought this war longer than anyone. People think that the rebellions rise up and are crushed only to be replaced but the truth is this is the same rebellion that was formed after the Gods left. Barwick is its leader."

"But what happens if you win the war?" Percival asked.

"The Gods may return," Caltrin said. "We hope so anyway. If we can somehow defeat the minions, the Gods may return to us and right all of the wrongs. That is why we fight. That is why I asked you to help me."

"Lord," Percival said. "I did not die to become part of a civil war."

"I know," Caltrin said. "But I fear you may not have a choice."

"Of course I have a choice," Percival said.

"I did not tell you this before," Caltrin said. "And maybe I should have. Maybe it would have been better if you had heard this first. Serpintus knows about you."

"What?"

"He knows that someone escorted Norhan and he found out it was you. He can find out who has died you see? And he found you out."

"And why should that bother me?"

"Because he's a vengeful bastard," Caltrin explained. "He'll track you down and torture and kill you."

Percival was silent for a moment and then said: "So if I don't fight for you I'll have to fight anyway?"

"Yes," Caltrin said. "Unless you hide."

It was unbelievable. Percival would be a fugitive because of a simple favor he had done for Barwick. He became angry once again at the thought of it. He was sure that if had not had to escort Norhan he would have been able to slip into the Otherworld without raising attention. Caltrin guessed what he was thinking however.

"It wouldn't have mattered if you didn't escort Norhan," he said. "Eventually Serpintus or one of his people would have committed some atrocity and you would have seen it and you would have fought. You wouldn't be able to help yourself. I know you, Percival. You would have fought."

Percival did not really believe that. The two walked down the magically lit tunnel in silence for a while. Caltrin was letting him think. Percival wanted so badly to believe that he could have a peaceful afterlife. It seemed however that it was not to be.

"You said something about hiding," Percival said.

"You can hide," Caltrin said. "But it is really imprisonment. Your very existence will be shallow."

"But you are in hiding," Percival said. "You're imprisoned in a way. How can you tell me anything different."

"There is one difference," Caltrin said. "We are fighting. We have been for years. It is better to be rebels, with the constant threat of being massacred in an ambush or attack than it is to be enslaved by Serpintus."

"I still don't know," Percival said.

"Percival, have I ever given you a reason to doubt me?"

"No, lord," Percival said.

"Then don't doubt me now. I beg you. Don't doubt me now. Besides, there is something you really need to know."

"What?"

"Palcron is a traitor."

"My Gods," Percival said. "Are you sure?"

"According to Barwick's spies in Serpintus' court, he is a traitor."

"And what does this have to do with me?" Percival asked, always suspicious.

"I want you to take over for me because he will hand the movement over to the minions. It will all be over."

"But surely there are better men."

"None," Caltrin said. "I trust you far more than I have ever trusted anyone else. I want you taking over for me."

Percival mused over this for a moment. His mind was ever calculating. He thought about what it would mean to take over and what the reaction of the rest of the army would be. He wondered if Barwick was alright with this. He wondered about his man Hullsham and what he would say to an upstart like Percival.

"What did Palcron say after I left?" he asked.

"He was outraged that I would select you to replace me. I told him some scheme that we already have assigned to someone else. I told him that it was what I wanted my replacement to do and now he thinks he's going to be doing it as commander of the army. We are planning to trap him."

"We?"

"Barwick and Hullsham and I are planning it. Once it's over I need a new second-in-command and if I die, we will need a new commander."

Chapter Six

The celestial warriors of the Gods, the angels, were the greatest threat to the minions. For that reason, the first battles in the War of the Gods occurred between the minion race and the angelic race. After humanity sided with the minions, the angels followed the Gods into exile, leaving humanity utterly defenseless.

The preparations for the battle were done in two contradicting ways. Caltrin made a show of only asking for volunteers to face the ever growing army of Serpintus but then in secret, he discussed the arrival of reinforcements with Barwick. Percival was always present during these conversations and from the way both people talked, Percival had a good idea of things that had happened recently in the war to get it to this point.

Serpintus had lost little ground to the rebel movement but Barwick had not made a full invasion of the Otherworld. There were rebel groups throughout Serpintus' realm ready to strike at a moment's notice. They had evaded detection for years and now they were going to be used. Barwick also had an army waiting to come to Riverbank. This army would be led by Hullsham, the leader directly under Barwick.

Barwick made a decision to trap Serpintus and Palcron at the same time. The rebels were hidden in a city that had little order. Serpintus believed that he had the movement cornered and was prepared to eradicate it. Barwick and Caltrin made sure that Palcron knew the rebels were defenseless from the massive army encamped outside the city. Palcron was surely relaying the information to Serpintus. The truth however was that there was a massive rebel army set to cross the River. This army would outnumber the overlord's.

The true essence of Barwick's plan was deception and it had supposedly worked up until this point. Barwick had secretly built a massive force hidden within the Otherworld. He had also built an army in the Savage Land that was evenly matched with Serpintus' army. The true size of Barwick's army was only known to a select few in the inner circle. Palcron was not aware of it. Indeed, he believed that the majority of the army had been massacred in a failed invasion. Therefore he assured Serpintus that the warband inside Riverbank was the last of Barwick's army. Serpintus gathered strength from the entire region and prepared to raise the city. He did not bring all of his forces but he brought enough to destroy the small number of the enemy he believed to be hiding in Riverbank. He brought enough to destroy Riverbank as well.

Palcron did not suspect a thing. He was to preoccupied to be suspicious. Serpintus had ordered him to find out where the prophet would be hidden. The problem with this was that Barwick seemed to be the only person who knew where Norhan would be kept. It was not unusual for the boatman to keep such secrets and Palcron thought nothing of being excluded from the knowledge. A day before the battle however, he found a definite lead.

Julron was angry that day. It seemed that he had been ordered to do something he did not want to do. Palcron overheard him saying that he didn't understand why he had to go into hiding with his sister and Norhan. Palcron then made it his mission to get Julron alone and speak to him about where he would be hidden.

"What seems to be the trouble?" Palcron asked Julron when he got the chance.

"Nothing, lord," Julron said.

"You don't like your orders, do you?"

"When I swore an oath to Caltrin and Barwick I thought I would get to do some fighting. Then they ordered me to go into hiding and guard Norhan."

"I think they want you as the last line of defense for the prophet. You're not seasoned enough to be on the frontlines."

"But I am wasted sitting around in the pit and you know it."

Triumph flashed in Palcron's eyes. He had him. The pit could really only refer to one thing. One of the tunnels that ran under Riverbank led to a secluded area with abandoned buildings. In one of those houses was a gaping hole fifty feet deep. It was a clever hiding place and could be easily reached once the overlord's army broke through the meager defenses of Caltrin. Palcron saw his reward well within reach.

"I will say you should trust the wisdom of Caltrin and Barwick," Palcron said, pretending to still be interested in what was troubling Julron. "Maybe they are saving you for some more important task later on."

Julron's face brightened up. "Do you think so?"

"I do," Palcron said. Then he walked away.

Not long after that conversation, Palcron sent a message to General Tragor with message powder. He said Tragor's name and threw the powder into the wind. He then spoke the message he wanted Tragor to hear. Tragor received the message in the form of a cloud of the powder that took the shape of Palcron. He did not send a reply.

¤

The war drums began to beat early on the day of the battle. Serpintus was ready to attack. Lines of men formed and prepared to march through the city gate. The gate was actually thick wood but it did not matter. Serpintus needed no battering ram to break through. There was a special kind of arrow that could burn the wood to ashes within minutes. It was one of the rare bits of magic he allowed his soldiers to use and it came in handy here.

The archers lined up behind the column of men who would march first. They fired their arrows and all hit home. The gate almost seemed to explode in flames. A cheer rose from the men and they began beating their shields with their spears. The echoing clatter made an evil rhythm meant to put fear into their enemies.

Serpintus took a deep breath. He was standing on a rock near the road. The rock was tall enough for him to be standing over his army. With his coat flapping in the wind he pointed a black finger and commanded his forces forward. The battle had begun.

Caltrin stood on the wall looking down at the army that would raise Riverbank. He had come to the wall to command the archers and to throw spells at the invaders. He noted fear on the faces of the men posted along the wall and tried to encourage them.

"Send their souls to the River, lads!" he cried. "Now get ready!"

The few archers on the wall pulled their arrows back and picked their targets. The gate burned beneath them and the sound of the spears crashing on the shields was almost deafening. Caltrin magically amplified his voice and ordered them to hold. The army below began filing toward the gate. It was beginning.

"Fire!" Caltrin roared.

Arrows rained down onto the overlord's army. Most hit their

mark. Half of the arrows killed. Those who were slain by the arrows flew to the River of Souls in cries of agony. Their bodies turned to dust upon being killed.

Caltrin ordered the archers to fire at will and then gripped his scepter tighter and ascended in the air. He hovered about twelve feet above the wall for a moment and then took his scepter in both hands and cast a bolt of energy into Serpintus' army. The bolt had the same effect as the magic arrows had had on the gate to Riverbank. There were cries of agony, surprise and rage. Then Caltrin rocketed toward the column of men in a blurring speed and left a hole of dead dust where armored men had stood seconds before. The enemy looked for him but he was not within sight. He was a mile above them.

"Barwick," he said looking into the glass globe of the scepter.

"Yes?" Barwick's face appeared in the scepter.

"My magic is spent for the moment. They are coming. Be ready."

Barwick did not respond but Caltrin knew he had gotten the message. The first part of the strategy was over. Caltrin remained at his elevation and flew to where he would truly be commanding.

The few rebel soldiers who were in Riverbank at the time were posted at various strategic locations. They were dependent on the reinforcements that Barwick was bringing and so they all feared to begin fighting without them. Percival was in charge of the group that would hold the first city-square. He saw with thankfulness that most of the men he was commanding appeared to be battle-hardened warriors: seasoned spearmen who knew how to fight. He thought of how he had come to this point yet again. It was Caltrin who had brought him into the king's army and now it was Caltrin who brought him into the Gods' army. The shield-wall was his destiny. He had to accept that, at least for the time being. Perhaps this would be his last time in a shield-wall.

He heard the blasts of Caltrin's magic and knew that it had started. He took a deep breath and waited expectantly for the attackers who were sure to come. He felt the familiar fear that he always felt before a battle but there was another emotion there as well. There was excitement. He had not been able to fight in his last months of life, and though he said he hated war and told himself that he hated war, part of him craved the bloodlust that would possess him, that always possessed him in battle. He was, on some level, excited to be fighting once again.

His sword was at one hip and a dagger on the other. His spear was in his hand. His circular shield was on his arm, ready to join the shields of his fellow warriors in a thin phalanx. It was a bold move. They had to hold a narrow pass until help arrived. Once the reinforcements made it to the city-square, they were to fall back and join up in a new shield-wall that would decide the battle.

The enemy spearmen were charging through the gate. He could hear the shouts and war cries echoing through the city.

"They are coming!" Caltrin's magically amplified voice sounded from the sky. "They are coming. Be ready!"

A few minutes later Percival saw the first of the enemy appear on the road he was supposed to guard.

"Shield-wall!" Percival yelled. The shields of all the spearmen touched. Spears protruded from the front of the shield-wall like spikes. The enemy halted when they saw the shield-wall and erected one of their own. Now the standoff began. It took great courage or perhaps great foolishness to try to break an enemy's shield-wall. Most spearmen were content to stay in the safety of their own instead of attacking.

Percival looked the enemy over and wondered if the same battle rituals were present in the Otherworld as they were in the mortal world. Surely there may be a champion or simply a brave and fearsome warrior who would step out to challenge the leader of the band of rebels. Percival waited for someone to appear but no one came forward. At the moment they were at a stalemate.

Percival considered stepping out of the shield-wall and challenging someone to single combat but thought better of it. He would wait to see if any of the enemy followed the mortal traditions.

A man did step forward finally. Percival felt a little better seeing that battle traditions crossed the River of Souls like everything else. He could not feel much better though as he looked the man over. He was huge with a bald head and a deep scar on his face. When he stepped forward he dropped his shield and his spear. He then removed his leather breastplate and stripped to his waist and drew his sword. It was a great saber, jagged on both sides. It looked heavy but he swung it one-handed with ease.

The man walked as close to Percival's shield-wall as he dared and called out for a challenger. He berated the rebel spearmen, calling them worms and cowards. He boasted of the amount of enemies he had killed and promised to piss on the dust left by the rebels' bodies. Percival listened to him patiently for he knew it was all part of the ritual. Many of the rebel spearmen growled at the big man but none dared to go and face him. Most of the spearmen also knew it was only ritual. There was no fresh blood to get enraged and charge out into an untimely death. The boasts for the most part were falling on deaf ears.

Percival let the man strut about for a few more seconds and then decided he would face him. The man had turned away in disgust when no one had taken up his challenge and was walking back to his shield-wall when Percival stepped forward.

"Running away are you?" Percival asked.

The man turned back and glared at Percival. "From you, runt?" the man laughed. "Not likely."

Percival dropped his spear and drew his sword. He kept his shield on his arm. "Then you are more foolish than you look, and you don't look all that clever to begin with."

"Bastard!" the man snarled. He swung his sword a few times and then pointed it at Percival.

Percival stared fixedly at the man. He decided at the last moment to not use his shield, feeling it would be better to be able to move freely. He did not remove his armor or his helmet though he thought that it probably wouldn't protect him from the brute's blows.

For a moment they circled each other, neither willing to make the first move. The brute looked amused, as if he thought this fight would require little effort, as if there was no challenge in killing someone like Percival.

Percival struck first. He hacked at the man with a broad stroke. The man backed away from the blow and did not deliver a reply. Instead he waited for Percival's next strike which came immediately. The man parried the blow and began a series of quick strikes which backed Percival across the open area between the two warbands. Percival finally dodged one of the man's strikes and the strike was so hard that the man could not recover the force of the blow and Percival was able to escape the assault.

The brute growled in annoyance and swung his entire body around to where Percival stood. His sword was in his hand and his arm was extended to its full reach. As he turned, his sword cut through the air and came dangerously close to decapitating Percival who weakly parried and ducked at the same time.

Percival had a brief second to come up with a new strategy. An idea flashed in his mind and he knew he had to act on it. He loosed his grip on his sword during the parry and sure enough it was knocked from his hand. The overlord's warband cheered for their champion who roared in triumph. Percival was still low to the ground when the brute raised his sword to give the killing stroke. Just as he began to bring the blade down, Percival drew his dagger and lunged forward. He escaped the sword and plunged the dagger into the man's stomach. He withdrew it just as quickly and rammed it into the man's chest. The brute fell to his knees and dropped his sword. Percival took a step back to look at the injured man. He then stepped forward once again, and with one fluid motion, sliced into the man's throat. The man's crying soul could be heard flying to the River as his body turned to a pile of dust.

Percival returned to his cheering men, picking up and sheathing his sword, and retrieving his spear and shield in the process. He rejoined the shield-wall just as the enraged enemy began to charge.

The first of the enemy clashed with the shield-wall and were killed suddenly. That did not stop the next attacker who was also killed. Soon however, the enemy broke through and a hole in the wall was made. Percival's men fought bravely, killing and cursing their foes. Percival saw a man lunge into the hole and rewarded him with a spear thrust through the eyes. As the death-dust of the enemy piled up in front of the shield-wall, it became clear that they would be able to hold this narrow pass and keep Serpintus' men from the city-square until help arrived.

"Forward!" Percival cried when the enemy had fallen back. He wanted to gain ground on them and perhaps push them further away from the area he was to protect. The overlord's men were afraid of being massacred and fell back. They reformed their shield-wall and waited for the rebels to charge.

"Hold!" Percival growled at his men. The order was echoed by the other high-ranking men in the shield-wall. Percival knew that many of them were already consumed with bloodlust and were wanting nothing more than to kill.

Percival waited for a few moments and saw that there were reinforcements swelling the enemy warband. He wondered how long it would take for the real rebel army to arrive to reinforce him. The stalemate had resumed.

Serpintus flew above the city in the same fashion as Caltrin, only he gripped the hilt of his sword which was his instrument of magic. He saw that the rebel warband was condensed into one pass where they had nullified the numbers against them.

"Amusing," Serpintus said. He landed on the roof of a building not far from where the battle was taking place. He drew his sword and pointed it at the small rebel band. He was planning to cast a spell that would shatter the rebels' shield-wall and thus lead to their deaths. He summoned the energies to cast the precise spell and was so focused on that spell that he did not notice Caltrin sneak up on him. Caltrin hovered behind him in complete silence and when Serpintus cast the spell, Caltrin cast one of his own which hit Serpintus' arm and sent his spell hurling toward his own army. He cried in surprise and rage and he caught a glimpse of the spell breaking his army's shield-wall before he was attacked by Caltrin.

The magician rocketed at the overlord with blurring speed. Serpintus fell from the roof but stopped short of hitting the ground. He hovered for a moment and then looked to where he had been a moment earlier. There, he saw his enemy.

"Caltrin," he said through gritted teeth. He then flew upward, casting spells at the magician as he did. Caltrin deflected them and backed away. Serpintus landed on the roof where he had been and squared off against the magician. Without a word he cast a spell at him and Caltrin created an energy shield around himself, ricocheting the spell back at Serpintus.

"Our magic is on the same level then," Serpintus observed.

"It appears so," Caltrin said.

"But you know that you cannot win against me," Serpintus said. "Not even your magic can break my skin."

"Perhaps I can. Perhaps my magic is strong enough."

"Have you not suffered enough at my hands, Caltrin?" Serpintus said with a laugh in his voice. "Do you wish to lose your ears this time?"

The magic light in Caltrin's eye sockets flared like fire. He cast a bolt of energy from his scepter that struck Serpintus on the chest. As if to prove that the magic could not hurt him, Serpintus did not try to deflect it but took the blast.

Caltrin leapt into the air and flew through the city. Serpintus took the bait and followed. Thus, Caltrin led Serpintus away from the battle.

¤

Percival had no time to consider what had happened, no time to look up at the battle of magic between Caltrin and Serpintus. He saw the shield-wall break and urged his men forward.

"Forward! Kill them all!"

He speared a man in the face and withdrew his spear and thrust it into the neck of another man. He pulled it back out and came face to face with another enemy wearing a helmet with a slit for his eyes. Percival thrust his spear into that split with perfect speed and accuracy. Piles of corpse-dust were mixing together all around him and suddenly he felt the familiar bloodlust possess his spirit. He welcomed it.

He abandoned his spear and drew his sword. His shield took a blow from an enemy soldier but that soldier was cut down by a man at Percival's side. The broken shield-wall caused an elation among the rebels and a massacre of the overlord's army had begun. The joy of the slaughter was cut short however when Percival heard the horn. It sounded behind them in the distance.

"Fall back!" Percival called. Most of his men obeyed and began to retreat. A few however continued fighting. "Fall back, damn you!" Percival ordered again.

He led the men down the pass and into the city-square. Sure enough when they were in the square he saw the mass of reinforcements filing in.

"Shield-wall!" Percival called. His men formed a new wall of shields and spears to protect them until the reinforcements could assist them. Most of the spearmen coming into the city-square were on foot, but down one road there were armored horsemen galloping toward the battle. They rode under a banner of an eagle and Percival saw as they approached that the eagle was also painted on their breastplates. The man on the leading horse was clad in elaborate chainmail armor which was also embroidered with gold. Percival guessed that this man was Lord Hullsham and he was correct.

The overlord's army had filed into the city-square and were too disorganized to form a shield-wall. Hullsham led his horsemen forward and scattered the enemy even more. He had his sword drawn and he hacked down from side to side as he galloped among the panicked men.

"Kill them!" Hullsham called out to his men. The horsemen killed the scattered soldiers of the overlord with efficiency. Soon, however, the enemy began fighting back. Horses were killed as were their riders as more and more of the enemy filed into the city-square. When the horsemen retreated, the overlord's men formed their own shield-wall. Now for the moment they were safe for no horse would break a shield-wall. It would turn away at the last moment without fail.

There was a wide space between the two walls and another draw was beginning. Each side had felt the wrath of the other.

"Which of you is Percival?" Hullsham demanded when he had dismounted.

"I am, lord," Percival said stepping from his place in the shield-wall.

"My greetings and thanks to you, for holding as long as you did and not losing many men." Hullsham bowed his helmeted head slightly but made sure to keep eye contact with Percival.

"All are good men, lord," Percival said. "Battle-hardened I would suspect."

"That they are, my friend," Hullsham replied. "They have to be in this place."

A man from the enemy shield-wall stepped forward and challenged Hullsham to single combat. The man clearly wanted to avenge the honor of his army by facing and defeating a champion. Hullsham ignored him which angered the man even more and he cursed and spat trying to get attention.

"Pay him no mind," Hullsham said.

"I killed a champion earlier," Percival said.

"Did you now? No wonder this fellow's so angry."

"What news have you of Caltrin or Barwick?"

"Caltrin was being pursued by Serpintus, the last we knew," Hullsham said. "Barwick is going to try to intervene. I have another warband that will attack from outside the city when the overlord's men are all in. We will then surround them and slaughter them. Barwick's plan worked perfectly."

"So far," Percival said.

"I think this may be our big turning point. We may even figure out how to kill Serpintus."

There was an explosion on the other side of the city that shook the ground where Hullsham and Percival stood. Hullsham raised his head and looked in the direction of the blast as if he could see it from this distance.

"Caltrin must be fighting pretty hard," Hullsham said. "He had better hope his magic lasts."

¤

Caltrin was fighting for his life… or his afterlife, rather. Serpintus had closed in on him in a slum near the River. There was a narrow alleyway that Caltrin flew down which turned out to be a dead-end. He approached the brick wall that cut the alley short and instinctively launched himself upward while throwing a curse back at Serpintus. The curse hit Serpintus in the face and sent the overlord falling to the ground. Caltrin flipped once in the air and dove for Serpintus. He cast a devastating spell which caused an explosion that destroyed the entire slum. The blast was felt throughout the city. It even threw Caltrin higher into the air than he already was. When the smoke cleared however, he saw to his horror that Serpintus was standing on the rubble.

"Cute!" Serpintus yelled to Caltrin. "I wonder if you killed any innocents with that blast! I could just let you do that a few more times and do all of my work for me!"

Caltrin's eyes flashed to the boats on the shore. He saw Barwick's ships and on one of the docks he saw Barwick himself. He breathed a sigh of relief. Serpintus was already ascending to Caltrin's level so the magician hurled himself toward Barwick. Serpintus followed at the same speed and almost caught up with Caltrin. He did not see Barwick standing on the dock and did not realize what Caltrin was doing when he suddenly dove into the water. Just before he reached Barwick he dove out of the way, into the River. Then the speeding Serpintus met Barwick's fist. Serpintus was knocked all the way to the shore of the River by that punch. It was enough to hurt him as well. He looked up in confusion and then saw to his great anger that Barwick was running towards him.

Serpintus braced himself for the blow and managed to catch Barwick's fist. Barwick cursed and tried to pull free. Serpintus twisted his arm and then punched him twice in the stomach. Serpintus then let Barwick fall to the ground. He drew his sword and thrust it at Barwick. The boatman had a brief second to think about what was happening and why it was so strange. Barwick thought, "I'm a minion. He knows a sword can't hurt me. But what if it can?

Oh gods, it can." Barwick managed to roll out of the way as the sword bore down on him. The blade sliced into his arm confirming his suspicions that Serpintus' sword could hurt him. He grabbed a handful of dirt and flung it into Serpintus' eyes before leaping to his feet and stepping out of the sword's reach.

Serpintus was only incapacitated for a second. Soon his vision was clear and he saw that he had not completely missed Barwick. The boatman's arm was bleeding.

"It was designed to be a punishment to minions who disobey me," Serpintus said.

"It can break our skin," Barwick said to himself.

"I must thank you for choosing this city as the place of your rebellion's defeat, Barwick. I thought it might be another drawn out process.

"The end of the war is upon us, Serpintus. And you are about to lose."

"Fool!" Serpintus spat. "My army has already won! You'll go back to your boat and summon another rebellion in a century or two, but I'll have a time of peace."

Caltrin stood near the conversation, but just out of sight. He was tired of listening to Serpintus prattle on and on. He pointed his scepter at the overlord and unleashed a curse that he knew would not hurt him but may, instead, give Barwick an advantage.

Serpintus deflected the curse and twirled his sword to throw Barwick into the River. He then turned to where Caltrin stood and cast a spell. Green energy shot from the tip of the sword and hissed through the air. Caltrin cast a rebounding spell with his scepter that caught Serpintus' spell and thrust it back at him. The spell returned to Serpintus who instinctively raised his sword to block it. The spell hit the sword from where it had originated with a force that threw Serpintus back forty feet. There was the sound of breaking metal and when Serpintus stood up he saw that his sword had shattered.

Barwick leapt out of the water as Serpintus was cursing his ill luck. Serpintus looked up at Caltrin and Barwick who were closing in on him. Caltrin had the look of triumph in his eyes. It was surprised triumph but Serpintus could see the danger in his eyes. He made a quick decision and decided to vanish. He gripped the hilt of his sword with both hands. Only a small piece of blade was attached to it and he hoped that there was still enough magic to transport him to safety. There was enough and he vanished, transporting himself to his nearest keep.

Percival and Hullsham were leading their men in a thunderous charge. The other warband had circled around the city and had attacked the overlord's army from the other side. As they were trying to hold off this new attack, Percival and Hullsham saw it as their opportunity to finish the battle.

The enemy shield-wall broke and suddenly Percival was killing. He felt the great surge of bloodlust course through his soul as he killed and killed. His sword hacked and stabbed and he powdered the ground with the corpse-dust of the overlord's soldiers.

The two warbands cut into the enemy from both sides and then linked together. The surviving enemy fled through the city, pursued by blood crazed rebels. Percival and Hullsham attempted to call the men back but they both knew that it was useless.

A sigh of relief was felt throughout the rebel army who stood among the piles of corpse-dust. The battle was over and they were victorious.

"Victory!" a man cried out.

"Victory!" others called in reply.

"We have done it, Percival," Hullsham said. "Caltrin was right to trust you."

"Thank you, lord," Percival said.

Barwick and Caltrin had made their way into the city. It had been over two hours since Caltrin had destroyed Serpintus' sword.

Percival and Hullsham greeted them and Caltrin told them about the fight with Serpintus. They were thrilled to hear about the breaking of the sword. Caltrin quieted their praise however.

"We just came from the hiding place," Caltrin said. "The prophet is missing."

"No," Percival said.

"Along with Julron and Heleina," Barwick added.

"Palcron's missing too," Caltrin said.

"That treacherous bastard!" Hullsham growled.

"Come on," Barwick said. "There's no time for this. We need to make preparations to go back to the Savage Land. Serpintus will be back with greater numbers."

Chapter Seven

Minions are said to be invulnerable but that is not true. Their skin is so dense that it takes a lot of force and even magic to break it. The minions' bodies can be destroyed but they will not be trapped on the River of Souls. Their bodies begin reforming the moment they are destroyed. Therefore there is no true death for them, just a brutal pain that passes once their bodies are reformed. There is said to be a way to destroy the minions forever but it is believed to be a myth.

The battle was over and the overlord had lost. Palcron felt a sense of dread creep into his soul. He had told Serpintus wrong. That was what puzzled him. He hadn't told Serpintus the wrong thing. He relayed the information he obtained in the meetings. Caltrin and Barwick had said that Hullsham was too far away to be able to help and that there was no way to repel even a small army. Realization hit Palcron instantly. That was what they wanted him to hear. They knew he was betraying them and so they used him instead of executing him. They used him as a tool to lead Serpintus into a trap. The trap had been sprung perfectly.

He hoped however that bringing the prophet to the overlord would help make up for that failure. He had Norhan bound and escorted by three spearmen. It seemed that that part was easy at least. Norhan did not struggle. Really, what could he do? Palcron had overpowered Wulfric who did not yet know of his treachery. The spearmen kept the boy and the girl away. Norhan seemed amused by what was happening though and Palcron could not understand that. Did this prophet have so little fear of Serpintus that he could laugh at being captured? Palcron did not believe anyone could be that foolish.

Norhan walked in silence. Palcron was glad of this. He was worried that Norhan would call him a traitor and a coward which is what Palcron truly was. Though he was both of those things he did not like being reminded of it. He saw himself as doing what was necessary for his own survival and that allowed him to live with himself. Yet he feared a confrontation where he would be condemned as a coward.

"Lord," one of the spearmen said.

"Yes?" Palcron said. He had been walking a few yards ahead of the spearmen.

"We are being followed."

Palcron climbed a rock near the road and looked back toward the city. Sure enough there were three people on his trail. He narrowed his eyes in contemplation. It was the three he had left behind, Heleina and Julron, and leading them was Wulfric.

"I should have killed them," Palcron said. "But no matter. I'll kill them now."

¤

Wulfric had been foolish and he realized that now. He should have found a group of spearmen to help hunt down the treacherous Palcron. He also should have made sure that Heleina and Julron did not come along. He had only objected one time to them coming and they had ignored him. Wulfric had to focus on getting Norhan back so he let them tag along.

How clever Palcron had been. There had been cheers of victory echoing through the city. The elation and great relief was almost overwhelming. It was for this reason that the spearmen assigned to guard the only entrance to the hiding place had abandoned their posts. The hunt for enemy fugitives had begun and there had seemed no danger in abandoning their posts. The battle was over.

And then Palcron came. Wulfric saw him coming and went to greet him. There were spearmen with Palcron. Wulfric guessed their were some of Hullsham's men but he had been wrong. They were soldiers of the overlord who had donned the armor of the rebels. They subdued Wulfric while Palcron led the others into the hiding place and then left with Norhan.

One of the men who had been distracting Wulfric retreated. He and his companion had attacked Wulfric with their swords and it was all Wulfric could do to parry the blows. Though one of them retreated, the other was intent on finishing his work. It was no longer two against one however and Wulfric proved he was the superior warrior. Within a minute, Wulfric had ran his sword through the enemy's neck.

And then the chase began. Wulfric thought it would take too much time to find spearmen to help him take on Palcron so he chased the traitor himself.

Palcron and his spearmen had the higher ground leading to the mountain path. Wulfric saw them stop and he too stopped. He held a hand up for Julron and Heleina to stop and then waited. Palcron was now aware that he was being followed and Wulfric knew he would be dangerous.

Wulfric saw Palcron talking with one of his spearmen. The spearman took Norhan off to the side of the path while Palcron led the others down the slope.

"Hello, traitor," Wulfric said.

Palcron did not reply at first. He looked at the three and then laughed. "Didn't have the foresight to get any real help, Wulfric?"

Wulfric tapped his sword which was resting in its scabbard. "This is all the help I need to kill you."

"You always were an arrogant fool," Palcron said. "And you never gave any thought to strategy. You would just charge into any fight without worrying about whether or not you could win... How many men did you lose in that scrap outside of Norwelda?"

Wulfric narrowed his eyes but did not reply.

"This is why you never advanced. Why do you think you were supposed to stand guard duty? Caltrin didn't want to lose any more men because of a fool."

Wulfric growled in rage and drew his sword.

"Looks like the fool will now lose himself," Palcron said.

It was then that they were interrupted by the presence of a third party. Neither Palcron nor Wulfric nor any of those they were with had seen them.

"Lord Palcron," the leader of the party called.

Palcron turned and locked eyes with General Tragor. Tragor had five spearmen with him and he had his sword drawn.

"I am here to take the prophet to the overlord," Tragor said.

"I am taking him to the overlord," Palcron said.

"No," Tragor said. He pulled a scroll from a pouched he carried on his belt. He passed it to Palcron who unfolded it, scanned the writing, and rolled it up again.

"Damn," Palcron said.

"An order from the overlord that states I am to intercept you and bring the prophet to him." Tragor looked at Wulfric and his companions for the first time. "Did I interrupt something?"

"The prophet's protectors," Palcron said. "They came after him. I was just about to deal with them myself."

"They can come too," Tragor said. He then ordered his spearmen to arrest them. Wulfric fought at first but his sword was knocked away.

"Let's go," Tragor said.

"It's going to be a long walk," Palcron said.

"No it isn't," Tragor said. "We have the chariot just over a mile from here."

The chariot was waiting by a small lake. As Palcron set eyes upon it, his heart leapt. He had known of the chariots, had seen them in fact, but had never ridden in one. There were winged horses that would pull the chariots grazing on some grass as the small warband approached with their prisoners.

Tragor opened the door of the chariot and ushered everyone inside. There were nearly two dozen people all in all. The chariots were magical and could hold many more passengers than that.

"Will you be driving?" Palcron asked.

"No, the horses know the way."

Tragor climbed in last and the horses began to walk forward. The walk turned to a gallop and the gallop turned into a sprint. Then the horses were in the air, soaring toward the cloudless emerald sky.

Palcron felt a rush of energy course through his body. Flying was the most exhilarating thing he had ever done. He glanced around him. The prisoners had looks of fear on their faces. Some of the soldiers shared his elation. Tragor looked bored.

They could hear the beating of the wings growing faster as the horses sped toward their destination. Tragor said that the journey would probably take a few hours once the horses reached top speed. It was then that then that Palcron asked where exactly they were going. He had been under the impression that they would be rendezvousing with Serpintus in the nearest city that he still controlled. That would have taken only a few hours to reach on foot. Flying should take minutes.

"We are going to Norwelda," Tragor said.

Wulfric groaned and slouched in his seat. He sat up when

Palcron gave him an arrogant glance.

"Why there?" Palcron asked.

"The overlord wishes to make it a new capital. He is building a palace there and an amphitheatre. Rumor has it that it will be the largest arena in the Otherworld."

"An active amphitheatre," Palcron said with wonder. "I never thought I would see one."

"Oh, you will be seeing it," Tragor said. "It is almost finished."

"I remember stories about the amphitheatres. In the old days it was said that Serpintus had demons devour people for entertainment. Is he going to have demons again?"

"There will be demons," Tragor said. "He has people rounding them up. I daresay that after his defeat, he will want some entertainment."

"Now tell me," Palcron said. "Why did you come to take my prisoner?"

"The overlord asked me too," Tragor said, scratching his newly grown beard. "You see, after he was defeated he came to my mansion. He was not at all happy with you. He told me to find you and to make sure that the prophet was brought safely to Norwelda. He wrote the order, gave it to me, and then climbed into his own chariot and flew away." Tragor looked triumphant. He folded his hands on his lap and allowed himself a slight grin.

The horses' speed climbed steadily and they retained their top speed for the rest of the journey. After about two hours the horses began to slow down and descend.

"We are here," Tragor said.

They left the chariot and set foot on brick pavement. They were standing in an area where other chariots were parked. Spaces for chariots curved around in a semicircle. Directly across from where the chariots were parked was a stable that contained the winged horses. There was one opening in this circle. It was a small path that led into a road.

"We are in Norwelda," Palcron said.

"Yes," Tragor said. "In the palace stables, actually. We will be escorted to the overlord momentarily."

The escort came in the form of Serpintus' minion champion, Harwain. Harwain stood as tall as Serpintus but was completely bald. His hairline was barely visible and there was a curious black spot at its tip. He did not wear armor but was clad in a dark green tunic with black pants and boots. There was a sword in its scabbard at his side and that was his only weapon.

He greeted Tragor curtly and then led the way to the palace. It was obvious that he had no respect for Tragor. Few minions had respect for humans. The stables were not far from the entrance of the palace. Upon entering, Tragor ordered the prisoners to be taken to the dungeons. Then, as guards led Wulfric, Norhan, Heleina and Julron to their new living space, Tragor and Palcron were taken to Serpintus' court.

There was no one in the throne room other than Serpintus. He sat slouched in his great chair and clicked his armrest with his fingernails. His eyes narrowed to slits when he saw Tragor and Palcron.

"You are dismissed, Harwain," Serpintus said.

"My lord," Harwain said, bowing. He then turned and left.

"Did you bring me what I wanted, general?" Serpintus asked Tragor.

"The prophet is in the dungeons at this very moment," Tragor replied.

"Very good!" Serpintus said with sudden enthusiasm. His foul mood seemed to vanish and he sat upright and clasped his hands together. He was so excited that he almost jumped out of his chair.

"It is just as you requested, lord," Tragor said.

"And you'll be rewarded," Serpintus said. He then flicked his eyes to Palcron. Just as suddenly as he had sprung into his jubilant mood, he turned dark and menacing. "You," he said.

Palcron bowed his head and would not raise it again. He kept going over in his mind how everything had gone wrong for him. He had fouled up his betrayal so that those he betrayed would know his treachery and the side he joined would punish him for his failure. Palcron wished more than ever that he had never joined up with Barwick and Caltrin after his death.

"Perhaps Lord Palcron can explain to us why my army was massacred and I was made a fool today," Serpintus said.

"I was misinformed, lord," Palcron said.

"*I* was misinformed, lord," Serpintus mocked him. "What good are you? A traitor and a spy is supposed to give me a the upper hand. Wouldn't you agree, General Tragor?"

"Yes I would, lord," Tragor said. He felt bad for Palcron. He knew how it was to have Serpintus angry with you. He was, however, happy that Serpintus' wrath was targeted at Palcron instead of at him.

Palcron seemed to be on the verge of shaking in fear. Serpintus would only underscore Palcron's failure however. He raised hilt of his sword with its remaining broken shard of blade.

"I blame you for this," Serpintus said.

"My lord?" Palcron said.

"I remember having a conversation with you," Serpintus said with a far off look in his eyes. He looked toward the ceiling in remembrance. "You told me some wonderful things. You said that Caltrin had revealed to you that his scepter was not as powerful as my sword. You said that Caltrin feared a confrontation with me because his magic could not meet my own. What you told me made me believe I could destroy him myself.

"And do you know what happened? Do you know what happened as a result of my being *misinformed*? Do you know the humiliation I suffered at the hands of that arrogant magician?" Serpintus held up his broken sword and fixed his obsidian eyes on its fractured blade. "My sword. Broken because of you. You gave the rebels a great victory today."

"I humbly ask for your forgiveness," Palcron said.

"YOU ASK FOR MY FORGIVENESS?" Serpintus roared the question as he got to his feet. He stared unbelievingly at Palcron and then pointed a finger at him. "Do you think me one of your Gods?"

"No," Palcron said.

"Do you think that I have forgiveness inside of me? I do not have any forgiveness for you."

"No, lord," Palcron said.

"Therefore I pronounce judgment upon you," Serpintus said formally. "As you may have heard, I have erected a new amphitheatre for this city. You are going to be the first entertainment."

"Lord?"

"You will be fed to the demons when I decide to hold the first event. Until then, you will be kept in the dungeons."

"No, lord!" Palcron yelled in fear.

"Yes, Palcron," Serpintus said.

"No, no, no, no, no, no."

"Guards!" Serpintus barked.

Armed guards entered the throne room and waited for Serpintus' orders. The overlord told them to take Palcron to the dungeons and put him in chains. They put shackles on Palcron's wrists and nudged him toward the door leading to the dungeons. Palcron would not willingly move forward and ended up being dragged.

"No! No! No!" he cried as he was dragged through the door. "NO!" Then the door was closed.

Chapter Eight

The Otherworld was once a great utopian society of peace and contentment. Upon the disappearance of the Gods, the Otherworld began to mirror the mortal world. The minions let the order created by the Gods collapse. The misery of the mortal world was then present in the Otherworld, making existence a never-ending burden.

Percival was happy when the boat he was on finally came to the shore. He needed to get away from Riverbank. He had only been there a short time but it was long enough. The thought of living in a brutal continent like the Savage Land did not bother him. At least it would be far from Serpintus. He had seen what the overlord could do and he did not want to live in fear of it.

Percival stepped onto the sandy shores of the Savage Land. The first thing he noticed was the closeness of the forest which pressed toward the small strip of sand that made up the shore. Upon closer inspection he saw that there were some paths that led through the dark and thick forest. He had a sense of superstitious dread as he looked at the wall of trees.

"What's the matter, Percival?" Caltrin asked.

"Nothing, lord," Percival said. "Just a strange feeling."

"Well you are right to be a bit paranoid. There's danger here, though not as much as there is in Serpintus' land."

"What danger is that?"

"The demons mostly," Caltrin said while scratching his chin. "There's supposedly some mad people living in these woods too. I've never seen them though."

A group of spearmen came forward and held unlit torches in front of them. Caltrin, holding his scepter, magically lit the torches.

"We'll need the light," Caltrin said.

The spearmen went down one of the paths and Percival and Caltrin followed. More of the army followed behind, each had their torch come to life when they crossed into the shade of the forest. There was soon a long train of people moving through the forest, the only distinguishable feature was the torchlight. Neither Percival nor Caltrin carried a torch because of the light coming from Caltrin's scepter.

There were howls in the darkness. Percival looked left and right but could see nothing in the gloom.

"You won't see them," Caltrin said, "but they can see you."

The feeling of being watched crept over him. He told himself to not be foolish, that he only felt he was being watched because of what Caltrin had said, but the feeling was there. The noises in the shadows could have startled him. It took every bit of self-control he could muster to keep from flinching at the inhuman sounds.

"The really bad ones aren't this close to the water," Caltrin said. "These in the woods are no more dangerous than rabbits or squirrels. Some are a bit bigger though."

"How far away is the camp?"

"It's really not far. Maybe another two miles from where we are now."

It took another hour of walking. The progress through the darkened woods was slow but at last they made it those last two miles and came to a fortified village. There were torches on either side of a great wooden gate that stretched fifty feet. The fence on which the gate was attached surrounded the entire village. Percival could make out men sitting on the wall and guessed them to be archers keeping watch for intruders or demons.

A horn sounded beyond the wall and Percival realized that those keeping watch must have been waiting for the returning army. The gate opened slowly. The spearmen near the front moved out of the path just enough for Hullsham to come through. Hullsham beckoned Caltrin and Percival to follow him.

"We shall cross into my village as equals, as victors," he said.

They walked forward, side by side. Percival and Caltrin flanked Hullsham who strode into the village he ruled. There was a great applause at seeing him. He was a champion to these people, a symbol of hope against the minions. It was obvious by the look of pride in his eyes that he knew it.

Hullsham did not revel in this praise however. He gave a slight bow of his head and raised a gauntleted hand in a directionless wave. All the while he kept walking forward with Percival and Caltrin at his side.

The spearmen that followed the three into the village did enjoy the praise and glory that the villagers offered and they continued basking in it long after their leaders were locked away inside of a cabin.

It was Hullsham's home. It was small but cozy. There was a stove in the corner and a cot against the wall. There was a large round table in the center of the cabin with chairs encompassing it.

Hullsham said nothing but gestured with his hands that Caltrin do something. Caltrin, knowing what Hullsham meant, flicked his scepter at the table. Instantly shards of black blade appeared on its wooden surface.

"Thanks to you, Caltrin," Hullsham said, "we now have the means to be rid of the minions."

"That is all very well, lord," Caltrin said. "But though we have the tools we do not know where the place is that we may use them."

"Stop speaking so formally, magician!" Hullsham snapped in sudden irritation.

"Sorry," Caltrin said.

"Forgive me," Percival said. "But what does a broken sword have to do with killing the minions?"

"You don't know?" Hullsham asked.

"No," Percival said.

Hullsham looked at Caltrin who just shook his head. He then looked back at Percival. "I thought Caltrin or Barwick would have said something. It's my fault really. I should have had you in our meeting after the battle. You'd have learned of our new master plan."

"Which is?"

"It's risky and probably won't work," Hullsham said. "The plan is subtle. This blade on the table right here is the only blade that can pierce the skin of a minion."

Understanding seemed to come to Percival's face. "So you mean that with this we can kill the minions? We can kill Serpintus?"

"In theory, we can kill them... in a way," Caltrin said.

"Minions have died before," Hullsham said. "They don't stay dead though. They can... reform, so to speak. There is only one way to get rid of them for good and fortunately it is a simple task."

"What is it?"

Hullsham swallowed and then went on. "It was thought to be a legend but Barwick insists that it is true. The Dark Gods created the minions. They made them almost indestructible. There was one true weakness that they had and the Dark Gods made the weakness as a way of getting rid of the minions should they no longer need them. There is an island where the minions were created. This island has an altar. If the blood of a minion is spilled on that altar, all the minions will be destroyed instantly."

"Instantly?"

"Yes."

"And you know where this cave is?"

"Yes," Caltrin said. "According to all of the legends and stories and according to Barwick himself, the island is Golgotha."

Percival's eyes widened. Golgotha. That was an island in the mortal world which was supposedly connected to the Otherworld. None who ever went there returned. It was a dark place that had a constant swirling black cloud hovering above it. The aura near that island was frightening. No one went there anymore. It was said that there is a barrier to keep mortals away but Percival did not know if that was true since he had never met anyone mad enough to venture to that island.

"The greater problem that we face is getting to Golgotha," Caltrin explained. "Barwick has said that he has tried to go there by boat but the River of Souls won't go that far. It is only able to be reached by a secret doorway hidden somewhere in the Otherworld."

"But even if you could get there, what minion could you get to sacrifice himself?" Percival asked.

"The only one who ever became an individual," Hullsham replied.

"Sorry?"

"The boatman, Barwick."

"He would allow you to do this?"

"He has been searching for this cave for his entire existence really. He has wanted to die on the altar for nearly a thousand years."

"It makes sense to make him the sacrifice," Caltrin said. "All of them will die when the blood touches the altar, Barwick too. Even if he wasn't the one to die on it."

"But wait a moment," Percival said. "During the battle I saw people die. There were no corpses however, no blood. Everyone turned to dust. How can Barwick spill any blood on the altar? It will all be dust."

"That is a riddle that still has to be solved," Caltrin said.

"Quite right," Hullsham said. "Now we need to find a way to the cave before we set about to solve it."

"We all know who will tell us the path to the cave though," Caltrin said.

"Yes," Hullsham sighed. "I will be calling a meeting with all of our leaders tomorrow to discuss the possibilities of rescuing him."

"It's Norhan isn't it?" Percival asked.

"It is Norhan," Caltrin agreed. "He is supposed to solve all of the riddles with a great revelation, his final revelation. We're hoping that he doesn't do it where Serpintus can hear."

¤

Serpintus ordered his guards to fetch the prophet. The overlord was sitting down to a noonday meal when he decided that it was as good a time as any to speak to his most prized prisoner. Norhan emerged from the door to the dungeons a few minutes after Serpintus had made the order.

Serpintus motioned for Norhan to sit in a chair next to him. The overlord was sitting at the head of a long table. Norhan sat down and Serpintus told his guards to leave them.

"Are you hungry, Norhan?" Serpintus asked.

"No," Norhan said.

"Yes you are," Serpintus said. "I haven't had you fed since you arrived yesterday."

"I don't trust you," Norhan said.

"And why is that?" Serpintus asked. "Is it because of something you have seen? Why not tell me all about it?"

Norhan said nothing.

"What have you seen?" Serpintus asked in a voice of mild

curiosity. He sounded like he was merely trying to strike up a conversation with an acquaintance.

Norhan closed his eyes for a few seconds and then opened them again. He slowly reached across the table to the fruit bowl and selected what looked like an apple. He bit into it and sat back.

"You said you didn't trust me," Serpintus said.

"No I didn't."

"You looked into the future," Serpintus accused. "You saw that eating would not make you spill your secrets."

Norhan did not respond.

"It would, of course, make no sense for me to do that. I am told that you do not have the information that I want. You are supposed to receive it somehow."

"I have no idea what you are talking about."

"Do you know that I can make your afterlife very comfortable?"

"I am aware of this," Norhan said.

"I will do it," Serpintus said. "But I need something from you in order to do it."

"You want me, when the time comes, to betray my allies to you," Norhan said with an amused look on his face.

"Are they really your allies?" Serpintus asked before taking a drink from his goblet.

"You're not my ally," Norhan said.

"And how might you know that?" Serpintus asked.

"Allies don't capture each other," Norhan replied. "What are you? An idiot?"

Serpintus' eyes narrow to a glare but then reopened. Norhan could see the restrained anger on the overlord's face. Serpintus was not accustomed to taking disrespect from anyone, especially a human.

"They are most likely going to lose," Serpintus said trying to sound calm. "I offer you a chance at avoiding torture and pain. I will find out one way or the other. You might as well save yourself the grief."

"I think that you are terrified," Norhan said. "You have me brought before you to intimidate me. But I see through you. You believe if you convince me that there is no hope then I will tell you what you need to know without being tortured. You don't do this for me, though. You do this because you don't believe that torture will make me give up the information. You know that if you don't get this information then you will ultimately lose. And you cannot stand that possibility."

Serpintus regarded Norhan for a moment. He seemed to be in deep contemplation. As if he were playing a strategy game and had been forced to change his plans.

"Guards!" he suddenly yelled.

Guards emerged momentarily. They had been waiting at the entrances to the hall where Serpintus was taking his meal.

"Take the prophet back to the dungeon," Serpintus said. "We begin the torture sessions tonight."

¤

Heleina looked up when she heard the door open. In the dimly lit hallway she saw two guards escorting Norhan back to the cell. She did not move as her arms were chained to the stone wall. She couldn't even manage to look at the guards as they came in. She shut her eyes and turned her head away. This was strange behavior for her. She had always been strong-willed and rebellious. There was fear in her now that was not there when she faced her death at the hands of her father.

It was because of Serpintus.

She was terrified of the overlord. He had come to the cell one time and she saw the malicious look in his eyes. She knew there was something wrong with him. She sensed that he wanted nothing more than to listen to the screams of his prisoners. It was as if his sole purpose was to inflict misery on humans.

She knew that was the truth.

Norhan was walked into the cell and led to the shackles that were hanging on the wall. Norhan sat down obediently, held his arms up and waited to be chained.

"Thank you kindly, darling," Norhan said to one of the guards after the shackles were locked. That guard kicked Norhan in the chest as retaliation. Norhan bent forward as far as the shackles would allow him to go and coughed. The guards then left the cell and locked the iron gate behind them.

"Shouldn't have said that," Norhan said.

It took time for Norhan's eyes to adjust to the dim torchlight of the dungeon. When they did adjust he saw that Wulfric was strapped to a rack.

"Things have happened during my luncheon with Serpintus," Norhan said.

"The guards came and did it to him," Heleina said. "It was awful."

Wulfric moaned in pain for a moment and then was silent again. His tunic was open and there were deep cuts on his chest. It looked like his arms and legs were stretched to their limit.

Norhan looked around suddenly and realized that it was only Wulfric and Heleina in the cell.

"Julron's gone," Norhan said.

"Yes," Heleina said as she started to cry. "He was taken out of here shortly after you were. I don't know what they're doing to him."

Norhan thought of telling her not to worry about Julron, that the boy would be better than all right. Norhan had known this would happen and he knew what the next encounter with Julron would be like. The boy was not being tortured. He was swearing an oath of allegiance to Serpintus. He could have told Heleina this but he knew she wouldn't believe it. Worse, it would just upset her even more. It was better that she find out for herself.

Heleina let her weight rest on her wrists and ignored the pain from the shackles as they bit into her skin. "How did I get here," she asked. "I could be sitting in my house right now, waiting for the gardens to open to restock my food. But I'm here. How did I get here?"

Norhan felt a slight annoyance at her questions. She had asked them frequently since being captured. At first he felt sympathy and guilt for what had become of her but now his heart was hard.

"It was Fate that brought you here," Norhan said, reciting the tiresome consolation that he had repeated throughout his life. "There is a reason, and such... stuff."

True to Serpintus' word, the torture sessions began that very night. The overlord decided that he would carry out the torture himself. He came to the dungeons alone. He spoke not a word to Wulfric nor to Heleina and Norhan. Not at first anyway. He examined the crude rack on which Wulfric was attached and shook his head. None of the three spoke to Serpintus as he walked about the cell. It seemed that he was fascinated by every aspect of it for he spent a good deal of time inspecting it. In reality, he was only building the dreadful anticipation for what he had truly come here to do.

"I am going to make you tell me your vision when it comes to you," Serpintus said.

"Not likely," Norhan said.

Serpintus fixed his eyes on Norhan and touched the hilt of his sword. It was a new sword but it held the powers as the old one. Norhan expected that Serpintus would cast some enchantment over him. The overlord did not break his stare, but waited. He knew that Norhan was going to see what was about to happen and he wanted to read the shock on his face before he committed the act.

Norhan had not been looking into the future much lately because it was bleak. He knew there was not much to see and anyway, he had a basic overview of what was going to happen. It was like an outline in his mind. Small details he no longer knew but he knew enough of the big ones to keep track. Now the anticipation proved to be too much and he looked ahead. What he saw made his soul tremble with fear.

"No," he said.

"Oh yes," Serpintus said. "I don't think you'll obey me otherwise. This will show you that there is no victory in opposing me."

Serpintus' eyes flashed a crimson color as he tightened his grip on the hilt of the sword. The spell was cast but instead of Norhan experiencing the pain, Heleina did.

"Bastard!" Norhan spat. "You evil mongrel! You subhuman vermin!"

That was the wrong thing to say. Serpintus would let most taunts roll off his shoulders but the subhuman remark enraged him. He was not subhuman. He was far better than the humans. Who was this man to have an attitude of superiority?

While Heleina was screaming in pain and writhing back and forth on the wall, Serpintus came forward and struck Norhan across the face. The prophet's head fell back against the bricks and then he was unconscious. Serpintus then left the dungeon and returned to his luxurious palace.

When Norhan woke a few hours later he saw Heleina writhing in pain. Her voice was gone but her mouth was still open in a soundless scream. Norhan looked at her and asked himself if he could really let her go through this agony.

"It is not my choice," Norhan said to himself, "but it is necessary."

Norhan looked ahead. There he saw the future he had set into motion. If he played his part correctly, it would all work out. Of course that meant that he had to put those who might be his friends through agony.

"If you can hear me," Norhan said to the Gods who may have been watching, "please give me strength. I understand now. I know why I have this power. Now help me. Please help me."

Wulfric was awake and listening to Norhan praying. He tried to look at the prophet but his head could not turn far enough.

"Wulfric?" Norhan asked. "You have something on your mind?"

At first Wulfric said nothing. He just hung on the rack and took a few rapid and sharp breaths. Then: "You knew this would happen to her. To me."

"I did," Norhan said.

"How could you not have told us?"

"It was necessary for you and Heleina to be here. Everything that is about to happen will happen for a reason."

"For a reason," Wulfric said. There was a mocking tone in his wheezy voice.

"Indeed."

Wulfric said nothing else. Heleina continued to writhe in pain. Blood was streaming down her wrists as her shackles were cutting into her skin. Norhan could not imagine the pain she was going through. He knew that he would not be tortured like this. He also knew that the great revelation was fast approaching. He could not see what that revelation was. It was still blank to him.

Norhan focused his thoughts on the future and studied what was to happen. Hours passed while he did this and when he finally brought his consciousness back to the present he saw that Serpintus was standing before him once again.

"Welcome back," Serpintus said as the awareness returned to Norhan's eyes. "You have anything you would like to share?"

Norhan stared at Serpintus but did not respond.

The overlord considered Norhan for a moment and then tapped

the hilt of his sword. Heleina suddenly stopped flailing in pain and slumped against the wall. She passed out.

"You should thank me," Serpintus said to Norhan.

"Just shut up," Norhan said. "I have not had the revelation and even if I did, I would not reveal it."

"Not even if I torture you and everyone you care about?" Serpintus asked. "The pain that she just experienced is nothing compared to what I could do."

"I guess you will have to do your worst," Norhan said.

"Don't worry," Serpintus said. "I will."

He walked over to the rack and quickly scanned over Wulfric. He nodded his head and sighed. "I am going to be throwing Wulfric here to the demons in the amphitheatre," he said.

"I know," Norhan replied.

"I am sure that you do," Serpintus said. "Tell me something." He turned back to Norhan. "How will he die?"

"Fuck you."

"Very well," Serpintus said, turning to leave the dungeon. "I'll see you at the show, prophet!" he called back as he walked into the shadows and away from the prisoners.

¤

Norhan had to be rescued. That was the resolution that came about at the end of the meeting. Many of the rebel leaders were in attendance either in person or by message dust. Barwick was there by dust but he did not direct the meeting. He merely gave input when he felt it was needed. At the end, everyone at the meeting felt it had been foolish to give in to the prophet's absurd demands. He should have been dropped off in the Savage Land instead of in Riverbank. Barwick did put forward the suggestion that being captured may have been a part of Norhan's plan but the others were quick to point out that Norhan had never revealed the full extent of what his vision had shown. He had to be rescued and that meant going into Serpintus' realm, to a city where he saw still strong. Spies had confirmed that Norhan was in Norwelda.

"What we have come to then," Barwick said, "is a riddle. How do we retrieve Norhan from Serpintus?"

"Maybe we don't," Hullsham said. It was the first time in a while that he had spoken. What he said made the others exchange curious glances. There was nothing but puzzlement around the table.

"What do you mean, Lord Hullsham?" Barwick asked.

"We are safe where we are," Hullsham explained.

"Yes."

"We have villages all over these woods."

"So?"

"If we focus our energy on uniting these villages together we could form a kingdom. Why do we need Serpintus' Otherworld? We could make our own."

"What about the Gods?" Caltrin asked.

"I think by this time that the Gods may have decided to forget about us," Hullsham said. "I would have if I were them."

"And who might then become the king?" one of the spies asked. "You, Hullsham?"

"Who becomes king is unimportant. But maybe there is something to this idea. We could grow stronger and stronger over the years and then fight Serpintus on more even terms. Maybe we could outnumber him, eventually."

"That is a very ambitious goal," Barwick said. "But it has been tried before. There are too many people crossing the River. If I drop everyone here, we will get bad people, horrid people. It will become overcrowded and miserable. It will be the mortal world."

"Which is better than the Otherworld right now," Hullsham said.

"The last time we did this," Barwick explained, "it failed. The people fought amongst themselves and eventually, the kingdom that was formed was a ghost of itself. Trees grew around the ruins.

"I merely put forth the idea," Hullsham said. "It is up to all of us, and ultimately you, my lord Barwick, whether or not we act upon it."

Percival thought that Hullsham was trying to back out of the war. Being the designated ruler, he must have seen a throne in his future. If Serpintus was destroyed, Hullsham could be king of the Otherworld. However, there was the problem of getting to Golgotha and fighting through minions to get there. Percival saw the slyness with which Hullsham had proposed this idea. It would withdraw efforts from the war while building a throne in the Savage Land. Work on settling the jungle and then Serpintus' Otherworld will be irrelevant.

"Never mind that now," Barwick said to Hullsham, killing that topic of discussion. We need to get Norhan back."

"I volunteer myself for this job, my lord," Caltrin said.

"I'm counting on it," Barwick said. "I have no other magicians and I daresay that magic will be needed."

"We need a plan," Hullsham said.

"Caltrin and I can work that out," Barwick said. "I want Percival with you in the village. He will be in charge of the army while Caltrin and I focus on saving the prophet."

"You want me to run this army?" Percival asked, astonished.

"There's not much to do," Caltrin said. "Don't worry. It's not like in Armora where you will be marching on raids every harvest and fighting in open battlefields year after year. It's pretty quiet. You'll just be training our people to fight."

"And there is an impressive library here," Barwick put in. "You should like that."

Barwick and the others who were present by dust vanished, leaving only Percival, Caltrin, Hullsham and a handful of others around the table.

"I guess we are saving Norhan then," Hullsham said, concealing disappointment that his idea was shot down.

"I'll begin taking volunteers," Caltrin said.

"I will be meeting the men," Percival said. "Is there some kind of declaration of my leadership or something?"

"Yes," Hullsham said. "We'll show you to them so they know that you are their lord now."

The rebellion was close to becoming inactive once again but there was a small glimmer of hope. If Caltrin could retrieve Norhan, the fight could continue. If he failed, the rebels would spend countless years in the Savage Land, waiting for a new time to attack. Caltrin began preparing to go across the sea and save Norhan. It was going to be a daring mission.

Chapter Nine

There are goblins which inhabit the mortal world. These are the results of couplings between minions and humans. They are monstrous creatures who delight in mischief. A great campaign led by King Morlon nearly wiped them out. The existence of goblins is one of the few links between the mortal world and the Otherworld.

Caltrin had recruited a number of volunteers and had them prepared to set out for Norwelda. It was not only volunteers from Hullsham's village that were willing to go. Caltrin traveled to many other villages that dotted the forest of the Savage Land and from each he recruited men and women willing to help rescue Norhan.

Two days after the meeting with the leaders, a swamp-demon began terrorizing Hullsham's village. The swamp-demons were tall creatures with broad bodies. There were two horns on the back of their large heads and one on the tips of their snouts. They had tails with spikes on the ends and long claws on both hands.

Though their scaly skin and their imposing size made them seem powerful and tough, they were stupid and clumsy. They were also more vulnerable than most other demons.

A demon had entered the village undetected and had killed some of the livestock and injured one man. Percival led twelve men on a hunt for the demon. He had been told that they nested and traveled in packs. Percival had brought a guide who knew the woods and she led them to a nest where eight swamp-demons lived. There was a fight with swords and spears and arrows and then it was over. The only part of the fight that went ill happened to Percival himself. He tripped over a log and when he had gotten to his feet, one of the demons struck him across the face. He was wearing a helmet but one of the claws got past the mouth guard and cut into his skin.

Percival was poisoned.

The venom of a swamp-demon was paralyzing. The men and women in the small hunting party made a stretcher for Percival and carried him through the forest and back to the village. Once there, he was taken to the cabin of Morian, the physician.

Morian was an angry man. He had nothing but contempt for those around him. It was said that he had been one of the first in the rebellion after the minions took control. He had existed longer than most in the Otherworld. He was over six hundred years dead and he had so far avoided being turned into a ghost. Most who knew him, however, thought that he had become as mad as a ghost.

"Don't you know that swamp-demons are poisonous?" Morian asked when Percival had woken. "You almost died."

"You're Morian," Percival said. "The doctor."

"And you are a fool warrior," Morian replied. "Just charge in with your sword out and start hacking away and growling. Nothing can get past your armor. And when it does you expect me to drop everything to save you."

"Listen," Percival said. "I really don't feel like hearing this right now."

"I know. You think I don't know how you feel? I know more about how you feel than you do. I am a doctor after all."

"Please be quiet."

"I doubt that I can."

Hullsham entered the cabin and bowed to Morian. "Doctor," he said.

"Hully," Morian replied.

Hullsham ignored the disrespect. "And how are you feeling Percival?"

"I have work to do. I need to get up."

"You're staying in bed, fool," Morian said.

"Listen to Morian," Hullsham said. "He knows what he's talking about. I just stopped in to see if you were awake. I will be on the road for a while. The way you dealt with the swamp-demons was impressive."

"Yes," Morian said. "He almost did it without being poisoned."

"That is enough," Hullsham said.

Morian spat and then walked across the room to attend to some potions on a table.

"Why do you let him get away with such behavior, lord?" Percival asked.

"It's because no one else can heal his wounded," Morian answered for Hullsham. "Isn't that right, Hully?"

"One day you may push your luck too far, doctor," Hullsham said.

"Ha!" Morian cackled. "I have no luck. I'm stuck with you fools. If you want to kill me then go ahead, Hully! The ghosts on the River would make for more stimulating company."

"I can take no more of him," Hullsham said to Percival. "I just wanted to see how you were and now I will be off. Get well fast, so you can get away from Morian."

Wulfric woke in a new cell. He was no longer on a rack, but lying on a cot. He sat up immediately and looked around the room. Norhan and Heleina were not there.

The pain throughout his body was so horrible he could not stand. A groan escaped his lips as he tried to roll over. He had to think for a moment. Where was he? How had he gotten here? He remembered learning that Norhan had known they would all be captured. Then what had happened? He had slept and then he had been tortured again. It was especially bad that time. He couldn't remember the end of it so he guessed that he had passed out. Had he slept until he had woken here? He did not remember waking up again after the last torture session. This had to be a new evil Serpintus had designed for him. He wondered what was happening to the others.

This cell was lit better than the other was. This was due to the fact that it was not in a dark dungeon. It was actually a room with barred windows that let in plenty of light. As Wulfric became more and more oriented he noticed other things about this cell. There were no shackles or chains on the walls. There was furniture that was not torture devices. The cot on which he slept was comfortable and there was a table against the wall. Wulfric saw that on that table was a piece of parchment. He cursed under his breath for he knew what he would have to do. That parchment might tell him where he was and why he was there. To get to it though would mean getting up. Every muscle in his body protested this but he knew that he had no choice.

"Get over it," he said to himself. "Get over it."

He did not instantly jump off of his cot. He lay there for a while trying to muster his strength and will. He finally tried to sit up and fell onto the floor. He grunted in pain and remained there for a time. His face and torso where on the floor. His hands were flat and in a position to support his weight. One of his legs was still on the cot. He moved that leg down to the floor and tried to push himself up. It was useless. He couldn't rise more than a few inches before his pain made him fall again. He narrowed his eyes and took a deep breath. Crawling was the only thing left to do and he knew it. He began slowly inching his way across the cell. Fiery pain coursed throughout his body and he tried his best to ignore it. It seemed that hours passed as he made his small, slow journey. At last he made it to the table. He ran his hand along the top and felt the parchment. Sighing in relief, he slipped the parchment off the table on onto the floor. He then rolled onto his back and held the parchment up to read.

The prophet has cracked.
Your resistance was meaningless.
You will no longer be tortured but will be nursed back to health.
No need to thank me.
-Lord Serpintus

Wulfric crumpled the parchment in his hands. He did not want to believe a word of what the overlord had written but he thought that it was very possible that Norhan had revealed the secrets of the revelation. Was that why he would be nursed back to health? Maybe that was part of the deal that Norhan had made.

No.

That could not be it. He would be a free man if it had been a part of the deal. If Norhan had told Serpintus everything he wanted to know, he had not made a deal on the behalf of Wulfric.

Could that mean that Norhan did not really reveal any secrets? Wulfric smoothed out the note and read it again. It did not exactly say that being made healthy was a result of Norhan cracking. The wording alluded to it but it did not say it exactly. Wulfric realized that Serpintus had another reason for healing him. There was something that he had in store for Wulfric that required him to be completely healthy.

"What does he want of me?" Wulfric asked to no one in particular.

He lay on the floor for a while and thought about going back to his bed. He was far too exhausted to move however. He fell asleep where he lay and woke hours later on the cot. There was no longer light coming through the barred windows as night had fallen. There seemed to be a dim and unnatural light in the room, a light similar to what Caltrin had created with his magic. Wulfric saw a new table by the cot. There was a loaf of bread, a cup, and a pitcher. Wulfric reached for the food and had his first meal since he left Riverbank.

The days stretched on and were all relatively the same. Wulfric ate three meals of bread and vegetables and drank pitchers of water. He was tended to by doctors who gave him different medications. His strength began to return and as it did he felt more and more defiant toward those keeping him prisoner.

The doctors would enter the cell escorted by guards. They would come when Wulfric was asleep and bind his arms and legs. Then, with Wulfric bound, awake, and angry, the doctors would begin the treatment.

"You know, someday I might get free and kill you all," Wulfric said.

"Not likely," one of the doctors replied.

He spent weeks being treated and throughout that time he received no word of Norhan or Heleina. His questions would go unanswered. He expected that Serpintus might come to the cell and gloat over his victory. He planned on asking the overlord about his companions and asking why he was being healed. He did not expect that Serpintus would be truthful. He thought that maybe inside the lies that he was known to tell may be hidden riddles that could be solved and reveal something similar to the truth.

But Serpintus did not come.

Wulfric began to realize that Serpintus had finished with him. There was only one thing left to happen and it would be the end. He knew that at the end of his treatment would be something far more horrible than anything he had so far experienced. That was the reason he was being nursed back to health. The state he was in after the rack would have made his final piece of hell far too brief. He knew that his transformation to a ghost would be long and excruciatingly painful.

¤

It had been a month since she had been imprisoned but Heleina did not know it. She had not kept track of time and she never knew whether it was night or day. Wulfric was gone and the only person in the cell with her was Norhan. She still did not know what had happened to Julron. When she asked Norhan if he could see Julron in the future, Norhan would ignore her or change the subject.

Since her first torture, she had only seen Serpintus one other time. He had come after Wulfric was gone and threatened Heleina in front of Norhan. She came to understand that Serpintus was targeting her in an attempt to get Norhan to tell him the revelation. Torture had become routine for her and Norhan. The main way that Norhan was tortured was being forced to watch as Heleina was stretched, whipped or cut. Serpintus did not oversee the torture but left it to his guards. The last time that they were tortured, Serpintus was there. He had come to the dungeon to talk to both of them in between bouts of pain. It was there that Heleina made her promise.

"I swear I will see you dead," she said.

Serpintus smiled and asked: "How do you plan to do that?"

"It will happen," she said. "I swear to all the Gods that are and that ever were that I will have revenge."

Now this should have sounded empty and meaningless. It seemed a very basic and vague threat but the tone in Heleina's voice chilled Serpintus and even chilled Heleina as well.

The torture session was once again uneventful. Serpintus left them alone for a while after that. Furthermore Heleina and Norhan were able to sleep on beds instead of hanging in shackles.

"Bad things are coming," Norhan said on the first day they were not tortured.

"You mean they aren't here already?" Heleina asked.

"No. It will get worse."

"What's coming, Norhan?"

Norhan swallowed and sat up. His hands were still bound though he was able to move freely about the cell. He placed his head in his hands and held that position for a moment. "Wulfric is going to be thrown to the demons."

"Oh, my Gods," she said. "So he's still alive then?"

"He is still alive. He will be thrown to the demons but I cannot see past that moment."

"Why not?"

Norhan looked at her and decided that he had to tell her his plan. This was the best time to do so. "I will receive my revelation at that moment."

"How? You said something would have to trigger it."

"Demon venom," Norhan said. "I will be struck."

"He's throwing you to them too!" she spat disgustedly.

"No," Norhan said. "I will be leaping into the arena to die."

"No!" Heleina yelled. "You can't do that!"

"I will do what I have to do," Norhan said. "It's about time that I'm done with it."

"How can you say something like that?"

"You have no idea what it's like. To know everything that will happen and everything that could have happened. It's the worst sort of existence."

Heleina did not respond. She would not have known how to respond to a statement like that. She had found herself envying Norhan's power to see the future but now she saw the downside. It was strange that she had never considered it before. Norhan was in agony. He was cursed and he wanted it to end. She supposed that she would want the same thing.

"So you don't know what happens to me then?" she asked after a while. "Or Julron?"

"I can't see what happens to you." Norhan said. "But I can sense things. It's strange. I know that I die and there's a blank beyond that point. I can sense that you escape. And so does Wulfric. Somehow, the information I receive is returned to Hullsham. I sense Caltrin will be present, somehow."

"What about Julron?" she asked.

"Never mind," Norhan said.

"No!" Heleina roared. "You have dodged this question every time I've asked it. What won't you tell me? What has happened to my brother?"

"Never mind."

"What has happened, you damned prophet?"

"He's betrayed us!" Norhan said in spite of himself.

"What?" All the anger left Heleina's face.

"I have seen him standing with Serpintus' men. He reveals to you that he swore an oath and that you will be saved because of it. You tell him about being tortured and he won't believe you. He'll harden his heart against you. Your brother is lost."

Heleina said nothing for a long time. Norhan cursed himself for revealing this. He had tried to avoid it for so long. There was nothing he could do now, however. He knew what was coming next. Heleina would be outraged. She would demand that he take back the outrageous lies he had told. Though they were not lies. Norhan knew this and Heleina, on some level, knew it too.

Sure enough, she began to accuse him of lying. She called him a cruel and evil demon with no soul. She demanded he tell her the truth about what was happening to Julron. Norhan fixed his stare on her and did not respond. After a short time of this, she began to understand that Norhan was telling the truth. Julron had talked more than once of swearing allegiance to Serpintus. It was not beyond him to do something like this. The more she thought about it she felt that it was actually likely.

"I am sorry," she said.

"Don't be."

"I shouldn't have called you those names. Shouldn't have attacked you like that."

"I shouldn't have revealed that to you the way I did. I am sorry about your brother. I don't know if he'll ever come back to our side though. But if it makes you feel better, I sense that it was supposed to happen. I think I can sense Fate and I truly feel that the things that are happening now are meant to be. Everything is falling into place."

The days dragged on and on but no guard came to torture them. The only person they saw was a servant who dropped off bread and water. Norhan elaborated on his theories of Fate and the feelings he had about the future. He revealed that things had to happen a certain way and if they didn't, everything would fall apart. Norhan was making sure things stayed on track no matter how horrid it may be. He looked forward to the day when he would end his existence. Then he would be free.

¤

Caltrin was eager to cross the River. He had his men ready to depart but Barwick seemed to be taking his time. He was supposed to leave an hour earlier but the boatman had sent a message saying he was delayed.

Caltrin had been busy these last few weeks. While Hullsham and Percival were trying to establish the rebels as a permanent threat, Caltrin had been recruiting volunteers to fetch back the man who might end the war. It was not a massive number since they would have to be covert. Caltrin would have to work an impressive magic to keep the small warband hidden until they reached the amphitheatre in Norwelda.

The amphitheatre had come as a surprise. It had been years since one had been used. They had once been active all over the Otherworld but they had been shut down after Serpintus became disinterested. Now it seemed that the overlord was revisiting an old hobby.

According to the spies, Wulfric was to be fed to arachna-demons. It would be a long and painful death if it was not prevented. A secret band of rebels were going to be hidden in the arena. That was going to be the strength of the battle. Caltrin would not be able to conceal a large amount of men so he had to rely on those he had never commanded. Barwick was optimistic but Caltrin was not.

On the shore of the Savage Land Caltrin's spearmen stood. There were only twelve including the magician himself. As the sun began to set Caltrin saw the silhouette of a ship in the distance.

"Our ride is here, boys," he said.

Barwick's boat ran ashore and the boatman beckoned them aboard. Caltrin and his men settled in and then they were off to rescue Norhan.

"I am sorry that I was delayed," Barwick said.

"Forget about it," Caltrin replied.

"This is truly difficult. I have divided myself too much. But there was nothing I could do. There were too many pickups to attend to."

"The others of you are working automatically though, right?" Caltrin asked.

"Not at this rate. My mind is moving among all of the different Barwicks. I have to focus to remain in this one talking to you."

"You are truly a screwed up man," Caltrin said.

"Yeah, thank you."

"Any word from your spy? Where do I meet him?"

"Everything is on the table in my cabin. I don't mean to be rude, Caltrin, but I really can't concentrate on talking to you."

"Of course," Caltrin said.

The magician opened the door to the cabins and descended into a hallway. At the very end was another door which was Barwick's cabin. Caltrin had grown accustomed to this room in his time serving under Barwick. He had first been brought there after his death, and from that day on he had been trusted of the boatman.

Caltrin felt weary of carrying the scepter. He felt this way from time to time since he was constantly carrying the magical weapon. He could set it down whenever he wanted but when he did, his sight vanished and he was blind. In order to keep the blue light in his empty eye sockets that allowed him to see he had to hold the scepter.

Entering Barwick's cabin he saw the papers on the table. He sat at one of the chairs and looked them over. He used the scepter to alter his sight to be able to read in the dim light of the room.

The spy's name was Issa. He was the leader of the group that would be under Caltrin's command once the battle started. Issa had confirmed that Wulfric would be the main entertainment. Norhan and Heleina were still prisoner and they were going to be forced to watch Wulfric die. Issa and his men would be able to be identified by a magical mark on their faces. The mark was invisible so Caltrin had to cast a spell on his warriors' eyes to allow them to see it. Only they would be able to identify Issa's men. Issa pledged himself and his men and women to Caltrin's command. In reality, he had pledged them to Barwick's orders. Issa was famous for his rebellious ways and pledging to obey someone he had never met must have been difficult. Issa had people who would grab Norhan and Heleina when the attack began. Wulfric would have to be saved during the battle if it was possible.

The pieces were set.

Caltrin's small warband was dropped off in Riverbank. A man

was waiting for them there.

"Lord Caltrin," the man said, bowing.

"Greetings," Caltrin replied.

"There are horses in the city-square. My lord Issa is eager to meet you."

"Is Issa here?"

"No," the man said. "He sent me to be your guide to our hideout. If you will follow me to the horses, we will be on our way."

Chapter Ten

Golgotha is a creation of the Dark Gods. When they came to the Otherworld, they needed a place to dwell in secret. They created the island in the mortal world where they believed that they would be left alone. They were for a time, but soon the Gods of the Otherworld began noticing the evil coming from that island. The Dark Gods were creating abominations in Golgotha. They were creating the minions.

It was the day of the event. The crowds were gathered and eagerly awaiting the show that Serpintus would bring them. The stands of the amphitheatre were filled to capacity with all of the depraved dead souls who took joy in seeing murder and mutilation. At the center was a wide open space where the entertainment would take place. The entire structure was oval shaped. At one end of the oval was a large gate designed for dramatic effect when the creatures were brought into the arena. At the other end was seating for the more noble people. Serpintus and his entourage occupied that place. With him were Heleina and Norhan.

"Do you feel excited?" Serpintus asked.

Neither responded. Serpintus said nothing more for a time.

The crowds were getting restless. Serpintus gave them a dismissive glance and saw that they were fighting amongst themselves. If that was what entertained the fools then let them do it, he thought. As soon as he turned his gaze away he shot it back around. Something had caught his attention. One of the said fools had struck another fool and dropped him onto the sand below. There was a cheer that could be heard, muffled by the sound of the crowd.

Serpintus was wanting to get things underway. He stepped onto the platform that stood out from his seating area. It was there for a noble person to address the crowd. It had been many years since a minion had done this.

"My people," he said with his magically amplified voice. It could be heard all around the arena. "I bring you what you want and what you love. Today you will see punishment for those who have dared to defy me. I punish them for your entertainment. As you may know, I have had some recent misfortune with that band of renegades led by that mad boatman, Barwick. These two men who will be punished today are directly linked to that loss. It proves that you may wound me, you may even humiliate me, but I will ultimately decide your fate. I rule over all of you. Someday I will bring all who have stood against me to equally horrible fates. Now I give you all the first round of entertainment. Here is Palcron!"

Serpintus returned to his seat. He crossed his legs, put his fingers together like a tent and watched intently as Palcron emerged from one of the secret passages along the walls. He was nearly naked and shaking with fear. He looked up at where Serpintus was sitting and begged for his life.

"Please, my lord," he sobbed. "I was a good servant. I gave you what you wanted."

Serpintus would not respond to Palcron. The pathetic man's pleas became incoherent as he tried to get the overlord to show mercy. Serpintus was not merciful.

It was Serpintus that opened the gate at the far end of the arena. He gripped the hilt of his sword and magically opened it as slow as he could. At first, only darkness could be seen where the steel gate had been. Then there was a growl. That growl was followed by another. Palcron crouched near a wall and tried to hide himself as the beasts emerged from the gate. It was two swamp-demons. They were large in frame but looked starved.

"No!" Palcron screamed as the swamp-demons set their eyes on him. He was on his feet instantly, all the madness from fear gone. The only thought in his mind was of survival. Looking around he saw nothing that could be used as a weapon. He saw the corpse-dust of the man who had fallen from the stands and wondered if maybe he had a knife in his clothes that could be used. Palcron almost ran for the pile of dust to rummage for a weapon but it was too late. The first swamp-demon pounced on it and slid out its long tongue to suck up the corpse-sand.

Palcron stepped back and considered his options. There were no options. This was the end. As he realized this, the cold, logical side of him began to vanish. It had nothing more to do. It was over for him. He began to tremble again.

The other swamp-demon attacked him, slashing with its long talons. Palcron's thin, sparse rags were poor armor to defend against such blows and the traitor fell over with deep cuts in his skin. The swamp-demon stopped for only a moment to give Palcron one last glance. Then it struck one last time and turned Palcron to dust. The swamp-demon's tongue went to work on collecting the corpse-sand.

"A splendid display," Serpintus said to the cheering crowd. "Oh, but there is more, my friends. You have seen a coward die defenseless but now you will see a warrior fight a demon with a sword and shield. It will be a thrilling battle but I do not like our little hero's chances. Behold, I will give you the warrior and the arachna-demon!"

The swamp-demons were summoned back to the gate that Serpintus reopened. Once they were gone he closed it again. He would wait for a while before he showed the main event. Wulfric's death would be long and painful despite the effort he put into the fight. Palcron's had been too easy though he had enjoyed it. How entertaining this was! He sat back and thought of all his enemies being devoured by the demons: Hullsham, the new one, Percival, and Caltrin. Oh, if he could only get Caltrin.

He did not realize however that Caltrin was not across the sea in the safety of the Savage Land. He was in the amphitheatre, watching and waiting for the right moment to humiliate Serpintus once again.

Caltrin and Issa had watched in silence as Palcron was killed by the swamp-demons. This was unexpected. Issa's intelligence had indicated that Wulfric would be the only one to be thrown to the demons. When Palcron was shaking so pathetically, Issa had asked Caltrin if they should begin their plan then.

"No," Caltrin said.

As Issa watched Caltrin watch Palcron die he could have sworn that the magic light that filled his eye sockets looked cold. He had been told that Caltrin had a cold soul but he was still shocked by the magician's indifference to Palcron's death.

"He was a traitor," Caltrin had said. "It is because of him that we have to rescue the prophet." This was supposed to explain his attitude to Issa but Issa still shuddered.

Two days before the event in the arena, Caltrin had met Issa for the first time. Issa was short and bald. He seemed to be a gruff man but people who got to know him found that he was rather jolly. He had clasped Caltrin's forearm to greet him and then he had pulled the magician in for a hug. This had surprised Caltrin who liked to keep his space from others.

"Thank you," Caltrin said, not really knowing what to say.

"It's an honor, Lord Caltrin," Issa said. "I've wanted to meet you for so long. The hero of the resistance, yes sir! Big fan of yours. Big fan. I was thrilled to be told that I would be working with you. I told that bastard on the boat that I didn't care how dangerous the mission was as long as I got to fight alongside my idol: you."

"Well that is very kind of you," Caltrin said, feeling a bit strange to be receiving such praise from a man he did not know. "I thought you would be resentful of me taking command."

"Normally, yes!" Issa said. "But I know about you. I welcome your leadership. I'll wager I can learn something from it, that I do."

"Okay. Let's get started then."

"Walk with me to my house and we will lay out everything. Imagine, Caltrin the magician at my table."

They were now inside of Norwelda and Caltrin was wishing that Issa would not announce whom he was having to tea. He wondered briefly how good a spy Issa could be when he seemed as subtle as a drunk in a whorehouse. He soon learned that his doubts were pointless. Inside Issa's house, he was shown papers that listed known minions in the city, the new recruits for the human portion of Serpintus' army, and transcripts of conversations that Serpintus had had in the past month. There were entire bound books on the shelves of this house that were filled with other information but none that was useful at the moment.

"We have someone who can copy the transcripts. He delivers to me every week." Issa was rather proud of that accomplishment.

"This is very impressive," Caltrin said. His eyes scanned over the new recruits and saw Julron's name listed. His face hardened for a moment and then relaxed. There was nothing he could do about that now. The boy had made his own choice.

"Norwelda is getting more popular with the minions," Issa said. "We don't know why."

"Serpintus has been more active here lately," Caltrin said. "Minions stay close to Serpintus out of habit. They tend to be obedient to their hierarchies."

"Except for Barwick," Issa said.

"Yes," Caltrin said, looking up from the papers. "Except for

Barwick."

"I'll have my people scattered in the stands," Issa said.

"How many will you have?"

"Thirty."

"Plus me and my eleven will make forty-two," Caltrin said. "I'm not sure it will be enough."

Issa picked up a stack of papers on the table and sorted through them. "We'll have enough if things go as planned." He showed Caltrin the blueprints for the amphitheatre. "Here," he said, pointing at the paper, "is where the spearmen will be watching. The way I see it, they're our biggest obstacle, so they are. If you hit it hard enough with a spell, you could kill or trap most of them. Then we save the prophet and run away. Should be fun or something close to it, so I think."

"That's an interesting plan," Caltrin said.

"I like it a lot, myself," Issa replied.

"It's still dangerous," Caltrin said.

"Because there's going to be a riot and we'll have to take care not to kill any innocent people."

"None of them are innocent," Caltrin said. "They are groveling to Serpintus because he's giving them this evil entertainment. If they get in my way, it's their problem."

Now here they were at the event, watching and waiting. Wulfric had been announced as the next act and Caltrin began feeling agitated. He was ready to get started and get out of there. He saw the balcony from which Serpintus addressed the crowd and guessed that Norhan was up there.

"I will be destroying the soldiers' section," Caltrin said to Issa. "I'll do it once Wulfric is on the sand. When that happens, you and your men need to be ready. I'll throw another blast at the balcony and hopefully I can clear a path to Norhan. It will get bloody."

"My men can handle it, so they can."

A door on the wall opened and Wulfric walked out, totally resigned to his fate. He was not a coward like Palcron. He was defiant. He walked out to the center and turned to look at the balcony. He stared up at Serpintus as if to show that he had nothing to fear.

"I'm going now," Caltrin said.

The magician, who had been wearing an oversized robe to conceal the scepter, leapt into the air. He shot two blasts from the scepter. One destroyed the section where Serpintus' soldiers were gathered and the other widened the balcony. Rubble fell to the arena floor. Wulfric looked at Caltrin with astonishment.

A riot began, just as was predicted. People were scared and were trying to get out of the stands before the mad man with the scepter could kill them. Caltrin made the oversized robe vanish and was then revealed in his full armor.

"Serpintus!" he roared.

The overlord was looking down in a mixture of surprise and calculation. The public punishment of Wulfric was not going as planned but he might still be able to win. He opened the great gate once again and this time, arachna-demons walked out. He was originally only going to use one demon on Wulfric for that would have been sufficient. He had four altogether and now he decided to release all of them at once. He would also bring out the swamp-demons. This was no longer entertainment. It was a new battle and Caltrin would be the loser.

Issa and his men removed their disguises and drew their swords. Some attempted to go through with their original plan and make their way to the balcony. Others, with Issa in the lead, tried to get to the arena floor to help Caltrin against the demons.

Caltrin seemed to be holding his own though. The arachna-demons were fearsome creatures, more so than the swamp-demons, but Caltrin's magic was enough to fight them off.

The arachna-demons had long bodies and stood taller that humans. They had eight legs, of course, and had horns on their heads just as the swamp-demons had. Their heads were large and they had gaping mouths from which they shot poison barbs. They had tails with spikes on the end. The spikes were filled with venom.

Caltrin was able to keep them at bay with ease. He had so far been unable to make a fatal blow but he had kept a barrier around himself. Serpintus saw from where he stood that Caltrin was not going to go down as easily as he had hoped. His face went cold when Caltrin successfully killed one of the swamp-demons.

The overlord knew what he had to do. He turned to one of this guards. "Guard the prophet," he said before drawing his sword and leaping into the battle.

Norhan looked at Heleina and she looked back. There was understanding in her eyes. Norhan leaned close to her to tell her what he needed to.

"I am leaping," he said with a whisper. "It's going to happen. I going to have my vision."

"But what then?" she whispered.

"Remember what happened at your house in Riverbank. Our minds are linked."

Just then, one of the guards broke them apart with a grunt. "You two think you're plotting something, do you? Stand over there, prophet. I don't trust you."

Norhan shuffled his feet to the place the guard had indicated and then turned to give Heleina one last look. He walked forward and stood on the ledge of the ruined balcony. Below him, the demons battled humans and the crowd of spectators tried to escape the crossfire. Serpintus and Caltrin were in the air, battling with their respective magical weapons.

"Hey!" one the guards yelled at Norhan. "Get back here, prophet!"

"No," Norhan said.

The guard drew his sword and started toward Norhan. The prophet looked down at the chaos below and ran forward. He leapt from the ledge.

Norhan landed on his arm, breaking it. He cried in pain and then put it out of his mind.He couldn't think about the pain though. He had to focus on Heleina's mind. He had looked into her future once and he hoped that was enough to link his mind to hers. An arachna-demon was in front of him. It had been fighting two people at the same time and had retreated to the place where Norhan lay. The demon saw Norhan and immediately twirled, slashing the prophet's stomach with the spikes on its tail.

Norhan, who had just stood before being struck, fell to his knees. His eyes rolled into his head as the poison coursed through his body. His mind was amplified for a brief moment and his powers doubled. He was receptive to that unseen force that whispered to all who could hear. He heard the whisper and the soft voice placed images in his mind. At first these images were random and chaotic. Then he saw them merge together like a puzzle. He saw the thing he was supposed to see. He saw the way to the place where the minions would be defeated.

The mountains. Specifically Arhanorgn which was concealed within the mountain range. The door was there. This door was unknown to everyone, even Serpintus. Norhan knew that though there was no real reason he should. The door led to a circle of rocks on an island in the mortal world. That circle of rocks was littered with human bones. The island was Golgotha.

Norhan focused on the images and played them in a steady stream. He prayed that the images would be transferred to Heleina's mind. Through the prophetic concentration he felt the aching pain from the poison taking control of his body. He was paralyzed. Distantly he heard Caltrin yell out the word, no, but he could not tell if Caltrin was referring to him or not.

"It's over," Norhan said. Though his voice was barely a raspy whisper, he heard a definite finality in it. "No more prophecy. Only madness." He felt no more pain. His body crumbled to dust and his spirit joined the others from the amphitheatre that were now soaring to the River of Souls. His ghost did not scream like the others. Instead it bellowed blood-chilling, maniacal laughter that could be heard over the sounds of battle.

Caltrin had watched in horror as Norhan leapt to his death. They had risked much to come here and were now caught up in battle in order to rescue that prophet and the damned fool had killed himself. Caltrin felt a mixture of loss and rage. If there was a way to call Norhan's soul back from the River and inflict pain upon it, Caltrin would have done it.

There was no time to dwell on this defeat. Caltrin had cast a lucky spell that had knocked Serpintus out of the air, and this had allowed him a chance to look over the battle. That was when he saw Norhan's death by arachna-demon. Now Serpintus had recovered and he was attacking.

Caltrin deflected the attack but had to drop altitude to avoid the next one.

"This is getting tiresome," Caltrin said, creating a shield with his scepter.

"I agree," Serpintus said in a mild voice.

A small black object rocketed toward them. Caltrin saw it first and ducked his head. The object hit Serpintus but glanced off his skin. The overlord caught it in his hand. Caltrin saw that it was a poison barb of an arachna-demon. Serpintus held it in his hand for a moment. He regarded it as if he thought there was something he could do with it but he had forgotten what it was. Caltrin tried to knock it out of his hand with a bolt of lightning from his scepter. Serpintus avoided the bolt and then snapped the barb in half. He threw one part at Caltrin. The magician shielded himself easily enough. Then he saw that Serpintus' face had brightened to a triumphant grin.

Caltrin knew not why the overlord was happy. He had deflected the feeble attack without much effort. He was unscathed. He then heard a cry from below and he recognized the voice as Issa's. He knew why the spy had cried out. His mind suddenly replayed the scene of Serpintus throwing the poison barb. He had broken it in half before he had thrown in and he only threw one piece at Caltrin. He had meant to distract Caltrin so he could not stop the other half of the barb from hitting Issa. Caltrin looked down and saw that Issa, who had been leading a group of men against the remaining arachna-demon had fallen. Caltrin's magical vision showed him the poison barb protruding from Issa's neck.

¤

Issa had fought bravely and expertly before being struck down by the barb. He bellowed commands at his men and organized them in the chaos that was the arena floor. It was luck that killed the first arachna-demon. It took a broken spear and an expert aim but one of his men, or perhaps it was Caltrin's, was able to throw the spear into the demon's gaping mouth.

"We know how to kill them!" Issa shouted. "Aim for the mouths. Stab them in the mouths for the love of the Gods."

The two swamp-demons were easier to kill than the arachna-demons. They had no armor coating like their eight-legged counterparts and could be speared or stabbed almost anywhere on their bodies.

There were three arachna-demons left. Spear throws were useless against them as they seemed to know their own weakness and kept their mouths closed.

"I don't see how we can kill them," one of the men said to Issa.

"I know. I think that first one we killed was the idiot of the bunch." Issa raised his shield to take a rain of poison barbs. "If only we had Caltrin."

But at that moment, Caltrin was fighting with Serpintus overhead. Just as Issa looked up at that fight, he saw the magician cast the spell that knocked Serpintus out of the air.

It was then that Issa saw Norhan jump from the ruined balcony.

"No!" Issa cried. "No. Get away!"

If the prophet heard, he made no reply. He got to his feet and took the blow from the arachna-demon. He fell to his knees, then he fell forward. He stiffened, lingered for a moment, and then turned to dust.

Serpintus had been watching in amazement when Norhan had died. His quick mind turned to Issa however. He saw Issa urge his men forward and watched as he organized attacks. Serpintus almost killed Issa right there but he thought Caltrin might intervene. Issa killed the arachna-demon that had killed Norhan by getting in close to the demon and driving a sword through its mouth. Serpintus again almost cast a killing spell but instead looked up and saw Caltrin hovering there, apparently in shock over what the prophet had done. Serpintus could not resist a chance to kill the magician and so took to the air again to try and kill Caltrin.

Issa and his men faced down the last two arachna-demons. Four demons were dead altogether and there was a strange attitude spreading among the men. They were still fearful but they were beginning to believe they could win this fight. As if to show this newfound optimism, one of the men in the shield-wall walked forward with only a small axe in his hand. One of the arachna-demons saw him and opened its mouth to shoot out poison barbs. The man was quick enough to dodge and to throw his axe at the same time. The axe became lodged in the arachna-demons throat and shortly after was sitting in a pile of dust.

The men cheered and then cornered the final demon. It was then that Issa had been struck by the poison barb. Issa cried out in surprise. He felt no pain. At least not at first. The pain crept slowly through his body. It began as a dull ache and soon transformed into a burning sensation.

Caltrin took his eyes from the battle and focused again on Serpintus. The overlord hovered before him with a look of smug triumph on his face.

"This was foolish," Serpintus said.

Caltrin did not respond.

"Your man down there is dying. That was clever of me, don't your think? You came for the prophet but the prophet betrayed you and your sacrifice. Now he's just a maddened spirit wandering the River as you will be."

"Not likely," Caltrin said.

"Fool! Look around. Those people down there are mine to kill unless you try to stop me. But if I kill you, I will kill them. If you flee and save yourself, I will still kill them. You cannot kill me. You have tried time and again. And now I think you will never be able to defeat me. The prophet never told you how."

Caltrin dropped to the ground like a stone, leaving Serpintus mystified for a brief moment. The action was so quick and unexpected that the overlord had to have a moment to figure out what had just happened. Caltrin broke off his fall before he hit the ground and flew like a missile at the arachna-demon. Serpintus was following at the same speed. Caltrin shot spell after spell to try kill the demon and then he collided with it. Serpintus halted where he was and hovered a foot above the sand. Caltrin and the demon fought but their movements were so fast that they blurred together. At last a cloud of dust formed around them and when it vanished, no one was there.

"I know that he can't be gone," Serpintus said.

Some of the men attacked the overlord but he paid them no notice. Arrows, spears and swords glanced off his skin as he watched Caltrin fight the demon. Now he turned his attention to the other men. With one swipe of his sword he sent four of them across the arena and slammed them against the wall. They turned to dust instantly. Then Serpintus descended to the ground.

"You men want to prove your skill?" he asked as he twirled his sword. "Take me on. All of you."

The men attacked at first but Serpintus beat them back. He was beginning to enjoy taunting them when he heard a rumbling noise. He turned his head and saw the walls of the arena crumbling around him.

"Caltrin," he hissed.

The magician was indeed causing the destruction. He passed through the walls and the stands of the amphitheatre with magical speed. The energy that surrounded him destroyed everything it touched. He moved so fast that even Serpintus' minion eyes could only see a white blur.

And then Caltrin appeared.

He emerged at a slower pace and cast a spell at Serpintus. The overlord was lifted into the air, and before he could cast a counterstrike, was thrown over the remaining wall of the amphitheatre. He landed on the stone road outside. As he looked upward he saw Caltrin soaring above him. He was pulling tons of stone from the wreckage of the amphitheatre into the sky with him. The stone was encased in an energy bubble that Caltrin opened directly above Serpintus. Tons of stone fell onto the overlord.

Caltrin returned to the sandy arena where the last of the men were still standing. He had purposely missed hitting any of them with the rocks and now they stood in shock. They had been inches from death every time Caltrin had destroyed something and now it seemed that they did not want to move for fear that the rocks might start flying again. Caltrin kneeled beside Issa and saw black veins running along his body.

"He's not going to make it much longer," Caltrin said. "He needs a doctor."

Caltrin told one of the men to call for Barwick and to have Morian waiting on the boat. He then said that he would be with them shortly after he dealt with one last piece of business.

Caltrin leapt up to the ruined balcony. There he saw Heleina and only Heleina.

"No guards?" Caltrin asked.

"They fled," she replied. She was not frightened. Indeed she seemed not to care at all. It was as if she was completely indifferent to what was happening around her.

"Okay," Caltrin said. "We need to get moving."

Caltrin's scepter glowed and revealed a message from Barwick directing him to send Issa ahead of them. According to the message, if Caltrin transported Issa magically to the River, Barwick would intercept him. Caltrin did this to the outrage of Issa's men.

"What did you just do?" They accused him. They thought he had killed their leader.

"I sent him ahead of us," Caltrin said. "Our doctor will look after him. Now let's get going. We are going to have a long journey and it will be dangerous. My magic is almost spent.

Caltrin found Wulfric was among the survivors and was glad to see him. They embraced like they old friends that they were.

"I am sorry that I failed you," Wulfric said.

"Never mind that now," Caltrin said. "We have to be on our way."

They found horses and were out of Norwelda before Serpintus woke and moved the rubble that entombed him. He thought of tracking them down and killing them all and then decided against it. His pride had been hurt in this fight. Caltrin had made him look foolish again. Serpintus would go to his palace and remain there for a time. After all, there was no one who could possibly defeat him and the other minions. His rule was safe and he was safe. He would let these humans have their victory today but he was confident that eventually he would kill them all.

Chapter Eleven

Caltrin's magic rivals the magic of Serpintus. However Caltrin must constantly absorb the magic around him. Therefore, there is a limit to his powers when in battle. If he depletes his magical energy he will be blind and vulnerable. Recently, Caltrin has been able to recharge much faster. This is due to discoveries he and Barwick have made in their research into the sorcery that binds the Otherworld.

Barwick picked up Caltrin and his companions on the shore of the River. He told them all not to worry about Issa. Morian had tended to him and had removed most of the poison. When everyone was onboard the boat and had been addressed, Barwick willed the ship into the water and set out for the Savage Land.

"What other news of back home?" Caltrin asked.

"Nothing really," Barwick said. "Hullsham and Percival have been working hard on fortifying the village. I've been dropping more dead off in the village. They are not at all happy with me when I do this but since we have been openly challenging Serpintus, I fear things may get dark on the Continent."

"You're only taking those you can trust right?"

"I am not a fool."

"Of course not."

The spearmen's spirits grew and they sang boastful war songs as they crossed the River. They began by laughing together and boasting of what each had done in the battle. Then out of the mixed voices of some rather obnoxious men, one voice was heard. It was a deep voice that boomed across the mess hall where the men were gathered. He was singing. He was the only one. It was a familiar song and soon more men began joining in until everyone was singing.

Caltrin heard them and smiled to himself. Everyone was celebrating victory even though they did not really have a victory. They had lost Norhan but they had overcome Serpintus. They did better than that. They made a fool of Serpintus. Such an accomplishment made them all feel victorious. Wulfric was even celebrating. The only person who did not seem to be happy was Heleina. Nor only was she not happy. She seemed to have no emotion whatsoever.

Caltrin opened the door of her cabin and saw that she was sitting on the floor with her back against the wall. He walked into the room and sat next to her. He made sure he kept a grip in the scepter as he sat so that his vision would remain.

"How are you doing?" Caltrin asked.

Heleina did not respond.

"Heleina?"

No response.

"Is it Julron?"

Still, there was no response.

Caltrin looked at her closely and saw that she seemed to be in a trancelike state. He moved his hand before her face but she showed no reaction. He then snapped his fingers. There was still no reaction.

"What did that monster do to you?" he asked. He stood and walked back to the door. As he opened it he heard Heleina speak.

"The mountain pass," she said.

"What?" Caltrin asked, turning back to her.

But there was no response. Heleina was gone again. Caltrin ran a hand through his hair and then left.

Barwick was on the deck right where Caltrin had left him. He stood with his arms behind his back, telekinetically guiding the ship.

"You have just been to Heleina's cabin," Barwick said.

"Yeah," Caltrin said. "Something's wrong with her. Something bad."

"I know. I'm going to have Morian take a look at her when we get back."

"Right," Caltrin said. "I am truly sorry that I failed."

"I know you are. I won't pretend that it is not a problem but we will get past it. There will be other opportunities to learn what we need to learn. At least, I believe there will be."

"But I am sorry."

"I know. But look at it this way, there's supposed to be three prophets. We'll get another chance."

After hours of travelling through mist shrouded water filled with the disembodied souls of the fallen, the ship ran aground on the shore of the Savage Land. There was a small reception to receive Caltrin and the surviving warriors. Percival was there but Hullsham was not.

As soon as Caltrin and company were off the boat, Barwick took to the River once again. Percival embraced Caltrin and the two walked together into the village.

"How is Issa?" Caltrin asked.

"He is well," Percival said. "Morian had him walking earlier."

"That's good. Gods, what a mess."

"I heard that Norhan died."

"The fool threw himself to the demons," Caltrin said. "He just jumped in and let them kill him. Everything we did was for nothing. All the people we lost. What a fool!"

"Lord," Percival said. "You did well. Wulfric and Heleina are safe. That's something, right?"

"Yeah, that's something. Now we have angered Serpintus, lost good warriors and have fled to the Savage Land where our rebellion will be silent while we continue studying clues for the doorway's whereabouts. But it's really something that we saved Wulfric and Heleina."

Issa was well. He was so healthy in fact that it was difficult for Caltrin to believe he had recently been paralyzed by an arachna-demon barb.

"How are you?" Caltrin asked.

"Better," Issa said. "Did you beat that bastard, Serpintus?"

"I did," Caltrin laughed. "We escaped before he woke up."

"Knew you were better than him, so I did." Issa sat up. He had been lying on a cot in Morian's cabin. "Could you hand me that?" he asked, indicating a small gray cup on the end table.

Caltrin handed it to him and Issa drank its contents in one swallow.

"What is it?" Caltrin asked.

"Don't know," Issa said with a belch. "The doctor said that I need to keep taking this shit to kill the poison, so he did. I don't feel the poison anymore though so I think it's all gone but he says it's not."

"Better to listen to Morian," Caltrin said. "He knows what he's talking about."

"That's right," Percival put in. "He cured me of swamp-demon poison.

"Who's this?" Issa asked Caltrin, indicating Percival.

"He's Percival. Hero of the Battle of Riverbank." Caltrin looked at his former second-in-command with pride.

"It's an honor, my lord, so it is," Issa said. He got to his feet and clasped Percival's arm.

Just then the cabin door was flung open and in walked Morian.

"Back to your cot, you fool!" Morian barked. He then began moving about the cabin, doing various tasks as he mocked Issa. "I walk out for ten minutes, just to drop off a prescription and then I come back and you are showering Percival with praises. Believe me, Percival is as big a fool as you. Got himself bit by a swamp-demon. Still want to call him lord? That's why he has such a big head. Aren't you two leaving?"

Issa sat back down. Percival opened the door for he and Caltrin to leave the cabin. "Oh!" Morian cried. "One more thing, Caltrin."

The magician stopped in the doorway.

"Hullsham has just had a meeting with some of the people still left in the civilized part of the world. He says that Serpintus is retaliating. He says it's going to be bad."

¤

Serpintus was indeed retaliating. In the hours since being defeated and humiliated by Caltrin, he began making preparations for a massacre unlike any seen in the Otherworld or the mortal world.

His personal warband was dug out of the rubble. Many had died when Caltrin brought it down but there were about a score of them still alive. Julron was one of them. The spearmen were all ordered to Serpintus' palace.

Message dust was spread across the Otherworld beckoning fellow minions to aid in the massacre. Every minion responded by agreeing. To save time, Serpintus had targeted every minion with the message. That meant that Barwick too would hear it. That was fine. He knew there was nothing the boatman could do. Knowing what was happening might even be painful for him.

It had been centuries since the minions had done something like this. That was because there was no real reason for them to band together to kill humans. The last time it happened was when Serpintus required a test of loyalty from them. He led them to decrease the Otherworld's population by fifty percent. He would aim higher this time. This time he was killing to prove the dominance of the minion race.

Serpintus knew that the minions would likely obey him no matter what he asked but he also knew that they would have a difficult time once the humans realized they were being exterminated. Therefore, the message Serpintus sent to the minions told them he would allow them to use the magical swords. Then they would have access to their innate sorcery.

Over the next weeks, the minions were equipped with the magical swords. The armies of the Otherworld united under their command.

Serpintus had left Norwelda for the city he viewed as his main capital. It was simply called the Center. It was located in the middle of the great continent that made up the whole of the civilized part of the Otherworld. In this city was great luxury. Serpintus spent a lot of his time there because he loved the city palace. It was the largest of his homes and had the most comfortable furnishings. It was from this place that he would command the massacre.

Serpintus ordered demons to be gathered in and released in every city. Not long after that order was given, demons began terrorizing the people. The people could fight back however, and though the demons killed many, they were unable to make a sizeable dent in the population. The demons were just the beginning. They were released to make Serpintus feel better until the minions could be gathered.

There was a place in the Center that the Gods had created. It was a room that had controls over every aspect of the Continent. Serpintus had not been in there in nearly three hundred years and when he entered it he wondered why he had stayed away so long. The room was a perfect circle and in the center was a blue beam. Serpintus stepped into the beam and immediately began hovering halfway between the floor and the ceiling. From there, he could control the Otherworld.

The first thing he did was spread the destruction of the gardens. The gardens could be dried up in two ways. Each garden had a pedestal in its center and in that pedestal was a key in the shape of a metal stake. Serpintus had pulled the keys in Riverbank and thus dried up those gardens. He would do it differently this time. From here, his mind could control the Continent as if it were parts of his own body. The gardens all across the Otherworld began dying. The only gardens left were the ones located in Serpintus' palaces. Those would provide food for the human army but the rest of the population of the Otherworld would no longer have a food source.

The overlord was not content to stop there. He began causing earthquakes from shore to shore. Clouds formed, blocking out the emerald sky. Storms rained down upon the people, violent storms that caused a massive death toll.

Only when Serpintus had had his fill of causing horrible natural disasters did he send his minions out to begin the slaughter. The people were defenseless. They had been plagued by demons, starvation, earthquakes and storms. There was no resistance as the minions led the human army from city to city, killing everything that moved.

The Center was in ruins within days of the great massacre's beginning. Serpintus decided to march toward the River after the Center was no more. He hoped that maybe Barwick's rebels would try and put up a fight. With three minions backing him as well as a massive force of humans, Serpintus knew that he would win. He wished that he would have gathered all of his strength before he fought Barwick and Caltrin in Riverbank but at that time he was stubbornly sure of himself. He had thought of himself as a god who did not need the other minions. He thought that all he needed was a small army and he could win. He had been wrong then and he had been wrong during the fight in the amphitheatre. Now he knew that it was better to have the other minions behind him. He still thought of himself as a god but instead of believing he had no need for the other minions, he convinced himself that their presence was part of his omnipotence.

The magic used to bring down the Center was some of the most extraordinary magic that Serpintus had ever used. He combined spells with his fellow minions and brought devastation upon the city. Buildings crumbled, sending the panicked people into the streets where they were rundown by horsemen or wiped out by an evil spell. Serpintus once again felt the great power he had known before his humiliating defeats. Once again he was the greatest being in the Otherworld.

War songs were chanted by the human soldiers who killed without mercy. The songs sounded like a death chant to the masses who were fleeing in fear.

Minions, leading their warbands, sacked cities and towns and then met each other on the warpath. The two groups of warriors would merge and become one massive army.

Yet through it all, no response came from the rebels in the Savage Land. Serpintus suspected that there would be no response since he was, for the first time in centuries, showing the enormity of his strength.

¤

Across the sea however, in the Savage Land, there was much unrest over what was happening. The rebels were demanding to be taken to the continent where they could meet Serpintus' forces. Hullsham refused. Caltrin refused. And Barwick would ignore every message he received from one of the rebels. They were not going anywhere.

"How can you do this?" one of the men demanded of Percival a week into the massacre.

"Don't be a bloody fool," Percival said. He was sitting in Hullsham's cabin, going over some papers when this angry man had barged in on him. Percival didn't take his eyes from his work as he talked.

"There are many over there suffering and dying and we won't do anything. I am not the fool here."

"You are indeed," Percival said. "We go over there and we die. We meet them head-on and we will be dead and the massacre will continue. I'll say that we are the reason that Serpintus is killing so many people right now and that is unfortunate and tragic. But we cannot stop it. We have to stay here."

"For how long? How long do we stay here and let this go unanswered."

"Decades if necessary."

"Damn you and damn Barwick!"

"You will hold your tongue," Percival said, rising to his feet. "I have allowed you to have your say and that is all you will have. Now you will obey our command or you will be banished to the forest. Is that understood?"

"Yes, lord," the man said.

"Good. Now leave me. I have work to do."

The argument had unsettled Percival though he tried not to show it. There was a deep sense of guilt inside of him. He felt that he was responsible for every person that was cut down. But there was nothing he could do to change it. Serpintus was taking vengeance on all of the humans while he was sitting safe in the Savage Land. There was nothing right about this. He had thought that perhaps Caltrin would gather the leaders and cross the sea where Serpintus would have them executed but Caltrin had made no such plans. If we die, Caltrin had explained, any hope of defeating the minions dies with us. It is a horrid situation but it is a test, a test that we must pass.

Where was Barwick?

The boatman had not set foot in the town since the massacre began. Percival knew that he had not turned himself over. He still made regular drop-offs on the shores of the Savage Land but he would not stay. As soon as the newly dead were off, the boat would vanish. Percival guessed that Barwick was feeling guiltier than any of them since he had been involved in the wars since the beginning. Caltrin had told Percival not to worry about Barwick. There was nothing to be done by worrying. They would have to live out their day-to-day lives and hope to learn how to destroy the minions before all of the Otherworld was destroyed.

Chapter Twelve

Though there has been much debate over the issue, no one knows where the Gods have gone.

Days turned to weeks and then to months before Serpintus' wrath was finally satisfied. By the time it was over his army had killed nearly half of the Otherworld. Serpintus had killed thirty percent before that with the catastrophes and demons.

The real difficulties were felt by the overlord's human army. When there were no minions to lead them, they had to rely on their own skills with sword and spear. Mostly they were triumphant but there were times when the commoners would beat a warband. News of that would travel and there would be a sense of resistance. The minions were quick to end that confidence however. All of them had Serpintus' magic and they were using it in the most malicious ways.

Corpse-dust filled the sky, creating fast-moving clouds that were pulled to the River. The towering structures of the various cities crumbled. The cities that Serpintus attacked himself suffered the most. The displays of the terrible magic were mesmerizing to the victims. Many would stare in awe at the spells weaved by Serpintus' sword. The awe would turn to horror as they died.

Julron was in Serpintus' warband. While on the march, he grew to regret his decision to join the overlord's army. He ran people through with his sword and spear. He killed without mercy. He did not want to do this but he knew that to disobey would mean his own death.. He hardened his heart against those he killed and ignored their pleas and their fearful stares. The killing did not get easier. In fact, it seemed to get harder the more he did it.

After he had participated in more murders than he could count, Julron decided that he had to get away. He had to retreat. Maybe he could make it to the Savage Land. The only way to do that was through Barwick. At the moment, Barwick was trying to bring refugees across the sea, into the Savage Land. Perhaps Julron could board one of the ships and cross.

On the day he decided to do this, Serpintus ordered his warband to the shore. There were people seeking escape there and Serpintus wanted them dead.

"I will be glad when this is over," General Tragor said to Julron during the march. The general had developed a liking for the boy since recruiting him. Julron liked Tragor as well and he figured that if they were not yet friends, they had to be close to it.

"Is it common that he does stuff like this?" Julron asked. "I mean: does Lord Serpintus make us kill like this a lot?"

"He hasn't done anything like this for hundreds of years," Tragor said. "It's that fool Caltrin's fault. You can't humiliate the overlord in two battles and not expect consequences. Hopefully, when this is all over, we will see no more of those damned rebels."

Julron's mind returned to the rebels. He had left them behind because he thought their quest was entirely in vain. He wanted to be wealthy, to exist in luxury. He wanted glory in battle and a place of honor in the Otherworld. He felt that he would be able to accomplish all of that in Serpintus' army. To him, staying with the rebels was foolish. He would have either died or continued to live poorly if he had stayed. He did not want to live among wild demons and he did not want to hide underground. He wanted to live above others. Furthermore, he wanted to save himself and his sister. In his infinite wisdom, he believed that there was no reason to pay for the crimes of the rebels. After they had been captured and Tragor had offered the boy a place in his warband, he knew he could finally realize his dream. He did not dream of bravery. He dreamed of glory. When the massacre began, he thought he might get a chance to win that glory. So far however, all he had won was shame.

"The cattle have all been herded to Riverbank," Tragor proclaimed to his warband. "We will join other warbands. The overlord is sending minions to join us and we will raise the city. This is it, my friends. This will be our final battle."

There was excitement among the warband at this news but Julron did not feel it. He felt bitter. He realized now that he hated himself, despised himself. He knew he was a thing of evil, something beyond despicable. He now thought that becoming a maddened spirit on the River was what he deserved. On that night, when Tragor announced the final battle would be at Riverbank, Julron contemplated ending his afterlife.

The warband stopped in the mountains. Julron climbed to one of the smaller peaks from where he could see Riverbank. There, just beyond Riverbank, was the River of Souls. Julron sighed as he looked at the River. He thought to himself that he could end it all. He could end his misery. He could spend eternity as a crazed ghost. At least he would no longer be aware of the terrible things he had done. He raised his foot and held it hovering past the edge. He tried to summon his will to make that step but the will would not come. He could not kill himself. Sighing once again, he brought his foot back.

"Not even brave enough for this," Julron said to himself.

"Looking over the battlefield," Tragor said from behind him. "I like to do that too."

"Feeling anxious, lord?" Julron asked.

"Not really," Tragor replied. "The minions will do most of the work for us. All we'll have to do is pick the rats off when they scatter."

Julron said nothing. Tragor wondered at the boy's attitude. He was not boasting of the kills he would make or singing old war songs like the other men. He seemed miserable.

"It is almost over," Tragor said. "I know that wars like this are difficult but I will make sure you are rewarded. I remember how you saved me. I don't forget things like that."

It was true that Julron had saved Tragor's life. It was during a raid on a small village. Tragor had been separated from the rest of the men and had encountered a blacksmith that had beaten him down. Julron had arrived just in time to see the blacksmith raise his hammer for the killing blow. Julron ran the blacksmith through with his sword, turning the man to corpse-dust. Tragor had expressed his gratitude and had promised to repay Julron when the time came.

"Come back down," Tragor said. "Rest until tomorrow. Then it's all over."

¤

Barwick had been taking people across the sea as fast as he could. He had rescued hundreds but still he felt each loss as a failure. He knew that many of the remaining people of the Otherworld were gathered at Riverbank and he resolved to attempt to rescue them. Of course, if he knew the people were at Riverbank, Serpintus knew it too. Barwick had to decide what the best course of action was. He could save a few by himself. There was no doubt about that but if he had help, he could save more.

Barwick crossed the sea.

He was received on the shore of the Savage Land by Lord Hullsham and Lord Caltrin. Barwick stepped off the ship and gave both men a brief glance before walking past them. He walked briskly down the path to the village with Hullsham and Caltrin following.

The large wooden gate was opened and Barwick strode into the village. The boatman ignored all of the greetings from the people. His eyes were focused on the cabin directly ahead of him. His pace was quick and it grew faster as he approached the cabin. The look of grim determination on his face made the people step away from him. He reached the cabin and flung the door open.

"Are you coming?" he barked at Hullsham and Caltrin who had been following at a distance.

"Coming, lord," Hullsham said.

Percival was in the cabin, sitting at the table.

"Get up," Barwick said.

Percival obeyed without a word. Barwick took the seat. Then he reached into his cloak and brought out a blank parchment that he unrolled and flattened on the table.

"I want," Barwick said, "people to help me in Riverbank."

There was no response.

"Most of the people remaining have retreated there. The city is overflowing with terrified people that Serpintus will attack soon. I can save some of them myself but if I have help, I can do a lot more."

"You realize what you're asking right?" Caltrin asked.

"Yes I do."

"And you are okay with asking this? You are okay with sending people to die?"

"Don't be a damned fool," Barwick growled at Caltrin. "What do you think this parchment is for? You think I'm about to write a poem here or something? Anyone who is willing to go can sign their name."

"You mean," Hullsham said, "anyone who is willing to sacrifice themselves."

"Quite," Barwick said.

"Count me in," Percival said.

"I figured as much," Barwick replied.

"I will go too," Caltrin said.

"No you won't." Barwick said, getting to his feet.

"Why not?" Caltrin demanded.

"You can't die. If you die then our plan will be completely unraveled. If we had another magician then I would let you come."

"I am not coming," Hullsham put in.

Percival flicked his eyes at Hullsham but then dropped his gaze just as fast. Hullsham's refusal to go to Riverbank seemed cowardly to him. But then, Hullsham was the designated ruler so perhaps he thought it better to remain in the Savage Land and look after his main responsibilities.

"That's fine," Barwick said. The boatman then paused and took a deep breath. "I am sorry that I am being short with you three. It's just all that I've seen recently is getting to me. All of those people... and there's nothing we can do for them."

"It is okay," Percival said. "We are all feeling the same way." Percival then signed his name on the parchment. "I say we gather everyone in the village square and announce our plans."

"Right," Barwick said. He got to his feet and led the three out of the cabin.

In two hours, a great crowd had gathered in the village square. In the center of the square was a platform, raised to the height of an average person. Barwick stood upon it flanked by Hullsham and Caltrin. Percival stood on the ground beside the platform.

"My friends," Barwick said. Caltrin magically amplified the boatman's voice. "This last year has been trying. Those we swore to save from the minions have been slaughtered because of us. But right now," he paused, "we have a chance to make a difference. It will be a small difference in comparison but we can make it nonetheless.

"The last of the survivors have gathered in Riverbank. As many of you know, I have been trying to take shiploads of people across the sea. That is what I intend to do now. I will race the ship back and forth, faster than I have ever gone. I need help. If we make a stand against the minions at Riverbank, I believe we can save most of the people."

There was a mute silence among the crowd. Everyone there knew what Barwick was asking.

"At this moment, my ships are travelling back and forth from the Savage Land," Barwick continued. "They are saving dozens at a time. Tonight I will put all of my power into the ships. I will save the maximum amount of people possible. I will do it with your help or without it. If I have your help though, I can do much more."

It was Percival's turn to speak. He had stayed on the ground to be at the same level as the crowd. The spell of voice amplification from Caltrin's scepter moved to envelop Percival as well.

"It is because of us," Percival said, "that these people are dying. We humiliated Serpintus twice since I crossed the River of Souls. Since he was unable to kill us, he killed the innocent.

"I have personally volunteered to lead this mission. I know full well that it is a suicide mission, as does our lord Barwick. That is why it is entirely voluntary. Any who wish to join the fight should write their names on the parchment in Hullsham's cabin. Know however that if you do decide to come, it will probably be the end of you."

During those hours after the meeting in the village square the people turned up to sign their names to the parchment. So many people signed up that they needed a dozen pages to hold all of the names. Those who did sign their names were equipped with spears, swords and shields. They donned chainmail and leather and prepared to board the ship.

Everyone was presented with weapons that had darker colored blades than usual. Percival was given a new sword and dagger. Each had blades that were almost black.

"Are these what I think they are?" Percival asked.

"Yes," Caltrin said from behind him. "They're finally done."

These new weapons that were being presented to everyone who signed up to go to Riverbank had been recently forged. Caltrin had helped a blacksmith melt down the shards of the sword that Serpintus had used in the Battle of Riverbank and the melted shards of blade were mixed with other molten metal. Caltrin began crafting swords, daggers, arrowheads and spearheads from that metal while a blacksmith hammered them smooth and sharpened them.

"These will kill minions," Caltrin said. "We tested on Barwick and were able to slice into his skin. Of course, minions don't stay dead. They'll reform and probably be angry but it should give you some help being able to be rid of them for a time."

The men and women who had signed the parchment were preparing to travel to the sight of their likely demise. Before the journey to Riverbank could begin however, a most unexpected event happened. A shriek was heard. The sound echoed through the village and was so loud that you would have thought it would be heard for miles around.

"What in the names of the Gods?" Caltrin said when the noise had stopped.

A moment later the shriek began again. Caltrin used his magic and listened for the source. When it was over he knew where to go.

"Come with me," Caltrin said to Percival. The magician then led his former second-in-command to a house at the far end of the village.

"This is Heleina's house," Percival said. And just as he said this, the shrieking began again.

Caltrin blew the door open and there, lying on the floor, was Heleina, and the shrieking was coming from her.

"What's wrong?" Caltrin yelled at her.

His voice could barely be heard over her earsplitting screams.

"SILENCE!" Caltrin roared, pointing the scepter at Heleina and nullifying the sound coming from her. She was still screaming but no one could hear her.

"This is beyond unnatural," Caltrin said.

"You're telling me," Percival replied.

"It's magic," Caltrin said. "She's under some kind of spell."

"But how? You didn't do this, right?"

"I didn't. It was probably Serpintus."

"That bastard," Percival said. Heleina was pounding her fists into the earth floor. Her mouth was still open in a silent scream.

"Wait a minute," Caltrin said.

"What?"

"She has been acting strange since her rescue."

"But that's been at least a year," Percival said. "I think the way she acts is the way she is now."

"But what if it's not? Suppose there is something that made her so withdrawn and miserable."

"Like what? A spell from Serpintus? Then why is it just now doing this?" Percival pointed at Heleina.

"Because it wasn't Serpintus," Caltrin said. "It was Norhan."

"Norhan?"

"Yes," Caltrin said. "Norhan had magic, of course. How else could he see the future? I have heard rumors that prophets can create visions in people's minds. Supposedly the visions can be in there but not be revealed for some time."

"You think that the screaming is because she's getting the visions?"

Caltrin didn't answer. Instead he pointed the scepter at Heleina's head. She had been writhing on the floor but now she stopped and stood. Caltrin lifted the silence charm. Heleina was no longer shrieking. Caltrin had control of her mind. He focused all of his concentration on searching her mind for the source of her madness.

"Found it," Caltrin said. Just as he said this, two ribbons of blue light emerged from the scepter. One attached to Heleina's head and the other to Caltrin's.

"I know what we have to do," Caltrin said when he had drained the images from Heleina's mind.

"What?" Percival asked. "I have no idea what's going on here."

"I have it in my head," Caltrin said. "Oh yes. This is a good day. Come with me."

They left Heleina's house and went back to Percival's cabin where Barwick was supposed to be.

"Should we leave her like that?" Percival asked. Heleina had fallen unconscious after the connection to the scepter was broken.

"She should be fine," Caltrin replied. "I'll send Morian to check on her later tonight. She had the vision the whole time but her mind couldn't process it since she had no magic of her own. But since I do, I can not only see it but control it and use it."

"Okay," Percival said with a confused voice.

"Don't you see what this means?" Caltrin asked. "Norhan was the first prophet and the actions of the first prophet are supposed to reveal the other two. Helen was the second prophet and I am the third. Plans have changed, Percival. We are going to end this war."

Caltrin flung the door of the cabin open with such force that he startled some of the people inside. Barwick wasn't startled. He lazily turned to look at Caltrin as the magician walked through the doorway.

"Lord Barwick," Caltrin said with excitement in his voice.

"What is it?" Barwick asked.

The blue of the magic energy that filled the magician's empty eye sockets grew a shade lighter. "I know how to get to Golgotha."

"How do you know that?" Barwick asked.

"Listen," Caltrin said. "Before Norhan died, he had his vision. He implanted it in Heleina's mind. That shrieking that you just heard, that was her. The visions were coming forward, overwhelming her mind. I took them from her. They are inside of my head now."

"All of them?" Barwick asked.

"All," Caltrin said. "I know what it is we have to do. I know how to get to Golgotha. We can end the war. We can end the minions."

Barwick rose from his seat and stood a pace away from Caltrin. He then grasped the magician's arms. "This is wonderful news," he said. "You must tell me everything you have seen. This changes everything."

The cabin cleared out except for Caltrin, Barwick, Hullsham and Percival. They were all silent except for Caltrin who was looking through the visions and deciding where to begin.

"I see a door in a mountain," Caltrin said. "Not in the mountainside. It is inside the mountain, in a cavern. It is a forgotten cavern, one not used for decades, maybe centuries. The door is hidden. Only a magician can find it. Or rather, it finds the magician. The door leads to Golgotha."

"Where is the cavern?" Barwick asked.

Caltrin did not answer that question but kept on reciting what he saw with his mind's eye. His grip on the scepter was tight and as a result, there was unintentional magic. When Caltrin went deeper into the visions, his eyes went from blue to pale white and a gust of wind blew through the cabin.

"Tragor will stop us. He is our biggest threat. It is not Serpintus nor is it any other minion. Tragor is the one who will stop us. He will kill me. Wait a moment. Norhan may have taken care of that."

"We'll deal with Tragor," Barwick said impatiently. "Where is the cavern? We need the bloody cavern!"

The earth beneath the cabin began to shake as Caltrin searched for the mountain's location. The shaking became so violent that everyone fell over except for Caltrin who began levitating.

"Arhanorgn," Caltrin said as the quake died away.

There was silence after this revelation. Caltrin came out of his self-induced trance and felt a great rush of relief. He was the third prophet of the Otherworld. The third prophet signaled the end of the minions. Everyone in that cabin knew that this was the end. One of the final signs had happened. There were so few signs from the one prophecy that it was awe-inspiring when they were fulfilled. That one prophecy had come true. The three prophets had come forward and the path to the minions' destruction was before them.

Arhanorgn. The mountain was deep inside the main continent of the Otherworld. Getting there would be difficult. It would also be foolish to suspect that Tragor, who had been indicated as the one who would stop them had been stopped. Even if Tragor was out of the way, the minions could still crush them.

"Okay," Percival said, breaking the silence. "We need to discuss what to do next."

"Agreed," Hullsham said. "Perhaps we should cancel the mission to Riverbank."

"That makes sense," Percival said. "We need to get to Arhanorgn, wherever that is."

"It's a mountain," Caltrin said. "It's a long journey."

"We need to send all of our strength to Arhanorgn then!" Percival said, slamming his fist into the palm of his hand. "Push through the minions and all of their soldiers and get Caltrin and Barwick into the mountain. If we get them to Golgotha, we win. That's all that matters."

"A lot will die," Hullsham said.

"But we could bring the Gods back!" Percival said. He was pacing back and forth now and an old fire inside of him had been rekindled. He hated the acts of war but he loved planning them. There was a rare joy inside of him now. He was playing a game of strategy. The Otherworld was laid out before him like a chessboard and he was arranging the pieces. "If we bring the Gods back," he said, "isn't it likely that They would restore everyone who sacrificed themselves to beat the minions?"

"Flawed logic," Hullsham said. "There's nothing saying They will return even if we kill the minions."

"It's not the point," Barwick said, finally joining the conversation. "We hope the Gods will return but They may not. The minions have to be killed. Then the Otherworld can be remade."

"So we push through then?" Percival said once again.

"No," Barwick said. "It requires more subtlety than that. Far more subtlety."

"I don't follow, lord," Percival said.

"We will help Riverbank as planned," Barwick said. "Meanwhile, Caltrin and I will travel to Arhanorgn under concealment. The minions will notice a massive warband moving through the land but they probably won't see a group of two."

"You think you both can make it to Arhanorgn?" Hullsham asked.

"I know we will make it," Barwick replied. "Our soldiers in Riverbank will be the distraction."

"That might work," Hullsham said.

"Of course it will work!" Barwick snapped.

"What about General Tragor?" Percival asked. "Should I seek him out in Riverbank and make sure he is killed?"

"Norhan says that has been taken care of," Caltrin said.

"That's right," Barwick said. "We should trust that for now and kill him if he does show up to interfere."

"So Riverbank is still on?" Percival asked.

"Yes," Barwick said. "But there will be some changes."

"Like what?"

"You are no longer leading our men into battle. Wulfric will do that."

"And what will I be doing?"

"I will be dropping off a separate warband somewhere else in the city. You will lead that one. I am hoping that together, both warbands will be able to push through the enemy and link together. You both need to keep them distracted long enough for us to reach Arhanorgn."

"Yes, lord."

"Now if Serpintus gets wind of what we are doing, he is likely to pull all of his strength out of Riverbank and come for us. If he does this, we will need help."

"Teleportation," Caltrin said.

"Exactly," Barwick said. "You have those things still don't you?"

"You mean the capsules?" Caltrin asked.

"Yes."

"I do. I don't have enough for an army but I can make some in no time."

"Right then," Barwick said. "If the minions learn what we're doing and they attack us, we will call for you. I want you all to be ready. When that happens, you will have to be transported to where we are."

"You bite down on the capsules," Caltrin said. "It will teleport you to us. You'll be drawn by the scepter."

"Now if there is nothing else," Barwick said, "I'll be preparing the boats."

The volunteers donned what armor was available. Some had chainmail but most had to be content with a leather breastplate. There were a few who had helmets and even less that had gauntlets. There were enough weapons to go around. Wulfric and Percival led their people down to the shore where three ships were waiting. Two of the ships were for the army attacking the minions in Riverbank first. The third ship, the one that Barwick and Caltrin were on, was for Percival's warband.

"Climb aboard and make it fast!" Barwick called out.

Once everyone was onboard, Barwick and Caltrin focused their combined magic and propelled the ships into the water and across the sea faster than they had ever gone.

Caltrin was talkative during the beginning of that voyage. He excitedly talked about revenge and finally Percival deduced that he was not talking about revenge for those being senselessly murdered.

"I am talking about my eyes," Caltrin said.

"You're going to finally tell me what happened?" Percival asked. He had tried to get Caltrin to tell the tale but the magician had always waved the question away.

"Two weeks into being dead," Caltrin said, "I confronted Serpintus. I was not powerful enough or skilled enough to win and he made short work of me. As punishment, he sliced out my eyes."

"I am sorry."

"I was a fool back then," Caltrin said. "I trained harder in sorcery. I have unlimited potential in the Otherworld so now I can fight him and beat him. Back then though, it was humiliating and painful."

"But we are going to win now," Percival said with great confidence.

"That we are," Caltrin said. "That we are."

The end of the war had begun.

Chapter Thirteen

Emissaries were the mortals who intervened between the Gods and the mortal world. They traveled about the nations proclaiming the will of the Gods. It has been centuries since the Gods abandoned the Otherworld but there are still Emissaries in the mortal world. Whether they are truly from the Gods or just religious fanatics is unknown.

The ships cut through the water and the wails of the maddened spirits. The journey took thirty minutes and the anticipation for what was to come was felt equally among the soldiers on the boats.

"I can't believe it is going to be over," Barwick said.

"You sound excited," Percival said. "But you are going to have to die."

"I want to die," Barwick said. "I've wanted to die since the Gods vanished."

"But why?" Percival asked. "I don't understand."

"We were created," Barwick said, referring to the minions, "by the Dark Gods. We were stronger than any of the other creations. The Gods of Light, who created the Otherworld, were going to destroy us. That was when humans began to side against the Gods. You see? The Dark Gods had not had a hand in the creation of the Otherworld but they created other things to undermine their rivals, which were the Gods we are trying to bring back."

"Okay," Percival said. "But why do you want to die?"

"I am getting to that," Barwick said. "I am a minion and I was once like Serpintus. I obeyed my orders without question. When the Gods abandoned the Otherworld, the angels went with them."

"The angels?"

"Yes," Barwick said. "There is a race of angels. They are powerful but we are more powerful. There was an angel who did not abandon the Otherworld. Her name was Ceresteil. She had this job before I did. She guided the souls of the dead to the Otherworld.

"I loved her. Do you understand that, Percival? I loved her."

"What happened to her then?" Percival asked.

"I was also a minion. Serpintus decided to test me. He commanded me to kill her."

"You obeyed, didn't you?"

"I obeyed," Barwick said. "Angels are not like minions. They can die. I fought to disobey but I couldn't. I killed Ceresteil."

Percival said nothing.

"When I saw her turn to dust, something snapped inside of me. I could stand against the other minions. I did just that. I went to Serpintus and I fought him. It was a stalemate though. I knew then that I had to do something to atone for what I had done. I had killed Ceresteil and more than that I had killed the person who could ferry the dead souls to the Otherworld. I walked into the water and I waited. I did not know what would happen, it just felt right. A ship rose out of the water in the distance. I swam to it and when I climbed aboard, I felt more powerful than I had ever felt. I guess that when I took over the boat, I received the power. From what I understand about it, the power is there but it requires a mind to guide it. My mind guides it now."

"But if you die," Percival said, "who will take the souls to the Otherworld?"

"I don't know," Barwick said. "The job will call someone. It will probably be someone in need of redemption like me."

"You want to die because you killed Ceresteil," Percival said.

"Yes."

"I understand."

Caltrin called for Barwick and Percival. The magician was standing on the deck and he had just seen smoke rising from Riverbank. Barwick and Percival ran up to the deck.

"My Gods," Percival said. There was a black cloud over the city that extended over the River, blocking out the emerald sky.

Caltrin touched his right temple and amplified his vision. "It's over," he said.

"That bastard Serpintus must have hastened the attack," Barwick said, spitting. "If we hadn't taken so long in the Savage Land... damn it!"

"What do we do?" Percival asked.

"What can we do?" Caltrin asked in response.

"We finish this," Barwick said. "We get rid of Serpintus."

¤

Serpintus was more than pleased with himself. Riverbank lay in ruins and its frightened people were being hunted down and killed. He knew it had been a good idea to begin the battle immediately. General Tragor had objected but Serpintus had waved away the objections. The men were tired but they did not have much work to do. Serpintus had led minions into the city where they cut down the desperate. Only then did the overlord order Tragor's men to kill all who remained.

It was finally over. All that remained were those in hiding but they would be dead when the food supply ran out. Serpintus determined that he would never again allow the gardens to produce food.

"We have done well," Serpintus said to the general. Tragor was the one human in all the Otherworld that Serpintus respected. He talked with Tragor as an equal and thought of him as a friend.

"Yes, lord." Tragor spoke while looking over the rubble.

"You and your men will be rewarded," Serpintus said.

"And then what?" Tragor asked. "Are we going to rebuild?"

"In time, I guess," Serpintus said. "I will make the Otherworld into a paradise for me and my followers. You will share in that, general."

"I wish we could cross the sea though. I would love to crush those bastards."

"Maybe in time," Serpintus said. "I think that could be my new project. If I can seize control of the Savage Land, I could take them out."

"What if you can't?"

"I don't think that it matters that much."

"Barwick won't bring people to the Continent though. Eventually, there will be a large kingdom over there. Then they will come."

"And you will be here to beat them back," Serpintus said with a smile. "Now walk with me."

They walked about the ruined city over which Tragor had once had lordship. It was remarkable how the structure of things that had been in place for centuries changed so rapidly. It was over a year since the Battle of Riverbank and the Otherworld had fallen. Things were truly different now and they would likely stay that way for years to come.

Serpintus had a hand clasped on the hilt of his sword. He too was reflecting on all of the changes in the past year and feeling proud of himself.

He heard a scuffling sound as he passed a pile of rubble. He stopped and stared at the rubble for a few moments. The pile was arranged in such a way that there was a space between the large pieces of stone. The overlord smiled to himself again and magically separated the rocks. A man bolted from the hiding place and ran as fast a he could away from the overlord and the general.

Serpintus drew his sword and twirled it in his hand. Then he swung it in the direction of the fleeing man. A green beam of light shot out of the tip and formed into an arrow that sped across the air and passed through the man's body, instantly killing him.

"Brilliant shot, lord!" Tragor exclaimed.

"The hunt after the battle is always more fun than the actual battle," Serpintus said, ignoring the general's praise. The most annoying thing about Tragor was his tendency to be a sycophant.

The men were rifling through the rubble that they could lift, in search of plunder. There was little treasure to be found however since Riverbank had been a poor city, and the people who had migrated here to be saved by Barwick had left all of their treasures behind.

"Lord Serpintus!" a man called out.

"Yes?" Serpintus responded. He was about a hundred yards from the man who had addressed him.

"I see ships!"

Serpintus leapt into the air and flew to where the man stood. The man then offered his glass to the overlord. Serpintus waved it away and the man collapsed it. Serpintus' eyes were sharp enough to see the ships in the distance. They were still dots to the humans but Serpintus could see them very clearly.

"Amusing," Serpintus said. "They came all this way, probably to make their stand and now they are too late." Serpintus drew his sword and shot three bolts of green lightning, one for each ship.

"Do you suppose they will attack, lord?" the man asked.

"Do you want them too?" Serpintus asked. His lightning bolts were drawn into Caltrin's scepter and there they were neutralized.

"I think we could fight them," the man replied. He was lying. The other minions had departed and only the human army was left. And that army was tired. There was doubt they could fight three shiploads of spearmen and win.

"I do not believe you will have to fight," Serpintus said. "They have nothing to fight for now. They'll turn around and run back to where they came from."

¤

At that moment, Barwick and Caltrin were in deep discussion about what to do next. They were arguing. Caltrin was furious. He wanted to attack the army at Riverbank right away. Barwick was talking calmly and coldly and that was furthering Caltrin's fury.

"I'll take on the bastard and keep him occupied," Caltrin said, referring to Serpintus.

"No," Barwick said.

"Why not?" Caltrin demanded. "Our men want to avenge those people. They died because of us! Let me lead them into battle."

"And if you die, all chances of defeating the minions will die with you."

"Cold hearted bastard," Caltrin grumbled under his breath.

"I heard that," Barwick said.

"Good."

"Don't be a damned fool. You know that I am right."

That was true, Caltrin thought, and the thought angered him. He wouldn't allow his mind to think logically. The logic was buried beneath the surface of his anger but he could still feel it and hear it. When he heard the logic speak to him it was as if someone else was talking inside of his mind.

Caltrin's scepter still glowed green from Serpintus' three spells. After the overlord had given a feeble attempt of an attack, Caltrin thought that maybe a real attack would follow. Percival had gone below to prepare the spearmen for a fight, should one begin. But Serpintus was no fool. He knew that Barwick ruled the River and any attack would be defeated.

"Where do we go next?" Caltrin asked, giving up his argument.

"The River goes deep into the Continent, as you know. The further it goes, the narrower it gets and that's where the danger is. We will be vulnerable."

"Well if we hurry there we may be able to get to the mountain before Serpintus realizes what we are doing."

Barwick vanished and appeared on one of the other ships. He summoned Wulfric to him and then outlined a new plan.

"I need you to lead the ships into battle in Riverbank," Barwick said.

"I thought that was what I was doing," Wulfric said.

"Riverbank is gone," Barwick said.

"I know."

"We know that Serpintus is still there. I want you to attack. Keep him occupied as long as you can to give us a chance."

"Fight until we die you mean," Wulfric said.

"Yes." Barwick stated the truth with cold simplicity.

"Very well," Wulfric said. "Make sure that you succeed though. Make sure that you get rid of the minion bastards."

¤

Serpintus had been wrong. The ships came to a complete stop on the River. The soldiers who had remained after the sacking of Riverbank saw the ships stop and watched them, unsure of what was about to happen.

Caltrin and Barwick combined their magic to begin this battle. It was a gambit but it was one that might give them an edge. Barwick projected his powers around one of the ships and Caltrin added his power to it and then they transported the spearmen in one of those ships into the midst of the enemy army in Riverbank.

The enemy was frightened and disorganized when Barwick's men appeared. It was so sudden and so fast that there was no time for them to form a shield-wall before the first spear thrusts began. Barwick's men were warned of disorientation before they were transported and they began fighting as they recovered.

It was a brawl.

Men were turned into corpse-dust as Barwick's soldiers avenged the atrocities of the past year. Eventually the rest of the enemy army joined their ambushed comrades and attacked the recently appeared warband.

"Shield-ring!" the leader of the ambush called. The spearmen then began forming a circle, touching their shields together but then Serpintus appeared, and with one swipe of his sword, he broke the loosely constructed shield-ring.

General Tragor's army charged, killing with a newfound strength. Serpintus lazily cast spells to offset the rebels but was content to let the humans do most of the fighting. He knew what was going to happen before it did. The appearance of the rebels was drawing all of the soldiers who had been busy seeking plunder a few moments earlier. They were now gathered in one spot to kill the rebels. Serpintus knew that another, larger warband would appear momentarily. That warband would not appear in the midst of the fight. They would appear somewhere close by and probably out of sight. Then they would charge in to break the overlord's warband.

That was exactly what happened.

The fight had taken place in low ground, which was lucky for

Barwick's men. They were unnoticed by everyone except Serpintus who did not care all too much. He knew he would win regardless of what happened at that moment.

The rebels charged. They ran down the not-too-steep slope with their shields raised and their spear shafts in their hands. A joint cry of rage and vengeance emerged from the men and women as they clashed with the enemy. Tragor's men were outflanked and crushed against the warriors in the broken shield-ring.

Spears stabbed into flesh that turned to dust. There were howls of pain and triumph across the small battlefield. The sound of sword bashing into shields echoed like a prayer to the Gods to return to Their heaven.

Serpintus drew his sword and almost began casting spells to end the fight. But then he stopped. Something was not right. This warband that had attacked was not very large. Three ships should have brought more warriors. He realized that the rebels were only from two of the ships.

"Where is the third?" Serpintus asked himself.

The overlord looked down and saw Wulfric in the midst of the battle. That man was quite brave. Not many would lead a suicide attack against the minion who had nearly tortured him into madness. Yet here was Wulfric, fighting hard and fast and killing without mercy.

"Tragor!" Serpintus called.

"Lord?" the general asked. He had killed the two rebels that were fighting him and was holding off another with his sword drawn.

Serpintus came down to the battlefield and killed the rebels near Tragor. "I want you with me, we're leaving."

"What about the men lord?"

"Don't worry, they'll beat the rebels. We need to go though."

"Can I bring men with me?"

"Fine, but meet me outside the city."

The general gathered a few men and they met the overlord outside of the city while the battle was still being fought. Tragor had left his second-in-command in charge saying he had received new orders from Serpintus. Then Tragor had found the few he wanted with him. Julron was one of those men.

"What is this about, lord?" Tragor asked Serpintus when they had arrived.

"The third ship," Serpintus said. "We are leaving now."

¤

Serpintus was no fool. He had an idea of why that third ship had not attacked. They knew something that he didn't. They were not throwing away their lives in vengeance but were sending themselves to die as a distraction. And it did not work.

"There is only one reason they would cross the sea now. And it is not dying at our hands as a form of penance for what they blame themselves for."

Serpintus paused and looked at the faces of the men that had come with him. None spoke, and it was clear that they were waiting in expectation for what the overlord had to say.

"They know how to win," Serpintus said.

"They can't," Tragor said. "The prophet is dead."

"There were supposed to be two more."

"No," Tragor said. "They can't know. They can't win."

"Exactly," Serpintus said. "We won't let them win. Let's go to Norwelda and we can figure out our next move from there."

Norwelda was full of minions that day. There were few humans left in the city. Serpintus came to his palace and sat in his throne where he could think quietly. Orders had been left to search out a warband making its way into the Continent.

¤

Julron felt a mixture of emotions over what Tragor had done. The general was only able to choose a few people to come with him and he had thought Julron to be worthy enough to join him. They were not a real warband, there were only six spearmen including Tragor. It appeared that Serpintus was going to give Tragor another assignment and a new group of soldiers to command. And Tragor wanted Julron at his side. This made the boy feel flattered and proud while also ashamed. He felt the shame in sharp contrast to the other feelings. It was due to his lack of resolve over what he should do next. It was like he was torn in two. One side of him wanted to stay with Tragor and gain in standing and maybe be a general one day. The other side told him what he truly needed to do. The selfish side spoke with his voice but this other side spoke with his sister's voice. The words came to his ears as clearly as if Heleina had spoken them. The words told him to betray Tragor and try to find redemption. Julron knew that it was not Heleina speaking through his mind, it was his own soul in turmoil and he had assigned her voice to be the opposing side. Julron had to make a choice and that choice would undoubtedly leave him with the feeling of loss.

He had been lost in thought all this time they were in the palace that he had no idea how long he had been standing outside of the throne room. Suddenly the golden doors were thrust open and Serpintus walked out slowly and calmly.

"There is another attack," Serpintus said with a gleam in his eye. "It's in Cateron."

"What is significant about that town?" Tragor asked.

"I don't know," Serpintus said. "All I know is that the last of our enemies are there. Now we can crush them."

Tragor assembled a small warband and Serpintus summoned what minions he could get to help. Then they went to battle in a small town just a few miles from the Center, to Cateron.

¤

Cateron was a town. It was not a city in comparison to Norwelda or Riverbank or the Center. It had no real value yet there was something about the town that seemed to draw humans like a magnet.

Now it was in ruins.

Percival led the charge into the city. He and his men entered and established a claim on it. They were not going to start killing people but they wanted to make their presence known. That way the attention would be on them and not on Caltrin and Barwick. This was a foolish gamble, in Percival's opinion. They were hoping that Serpintus would be occupied in Riverbank but if he did figure out that something was amiss he would think that the real attack was in Cateron.

"Just hurry up and don't fail," Percival had said to Caltrin before leaving the boat. Now he wondered if this would be the final stand. Perhaps it would all end here. Barwick would remain but everyone else would die. How long until another magician crosses the River of Souls? No. He would not let himself think like that. There was hope. This was the best chance that they had ever had of getting rid of Serpintus and the minions and they were taking it. Caltrin had proven he could stand against Serpintus, that he was even capable of greater magic. If he could do that, he could accomplish what he needed to accomplish.

It was not long after they arrived in the city that the minions discovered their presence. Percival looked out on the horizon where a dozen minions and their followers were flying through the sky like birds without wings.

So it was true that Serpintus had given the other minions magic.

"Archers!" Percival shouted, signaling a line of men and women with longbows to prepare their aims.

He waited to give the order. Make sure the bastards are too close to miss, he thought. Then, when the minions were close enough, Percival gave the order.

"Fire!" he yelled.

The archers fired. Their arrows soared through the air to hit their targets. The arrowheads, forged with pieces of the Dark Blade sliced through the armor and skin of the minions and turned them to dust instantly.

"We can hold them for a while!" Percival said. "Make sure your other weapons are ready!"

Minions fell before their eyes and their souls were sent to the River while they roared in rage. After their bodies reformed they did not return to the battle. Perhaps they were too humiliated to continue the fight.

Despite the arrows, some minions made it to the town and brought their human followers with them. The battle began the same way most battles did. Percival called for his men to form a shield-wall and then, with the phalanx formed, they stared down their minion enemies.

The minions were not foolish. They knew that these humans had the power to fight them and so they decided to step back and rely on their magic to save them. There had been seven minions leading this assault but only three had made it to Cateron. That number dropped to two when one of them was not paying attention. A throwing spear emerged from within Percival's shield-wall and found its target. The minion's face was alight with surprise and then with rage, not only with his attacker but with himself as well.

The last two minions began working magic against the rebels. One thrust his sword past the smooth stone pavement and into the earth below and caused a tear that toppled the carefully arranged men and women. After the shield-wall had begun to fall apart, the other minion cast a lightning spell that was drawn to all of the metal weapons. With these two spells, the shield-wall had been broken and the minions' human followers whooped for the joy of the slaughter as they closed in on their enemies.

The armies crashed together and Percival sunk his spear into the stomach of one man. He then dropped the spear and drew his sword. He heard a roar and looked up to see a big man screaming a challenge. The man had the eyes of a killer and muscles built by using his oversized sword. That sword was in his hand now and he brandished it menacingly. Percival looked at the man and managed to chuckle before he was forced to divert his attention to killing some other aggressor.

The big man was furious now. His eyes had bulged at the insult and that was what Percival had wanted. This man charged forward and killed soldier after soldier before he could get to Percival. He saw the banner of the angel on Percival's shield and breastplate and silently vowed to cover it in dust.

Percival growled at his people to fight harder and push back. He would not be overwhelmed even though a broken shield-wall was a terrible way to begin a battle. The rebels were ferocious and they were filling the air with enemy corpse-dust. All the while, Percival kept an eye on the big man who appeared to be a champion.

Finally, Percival was no longer able to avoid fighting the man and so he accepted this and turned around to face him. He was almost decapitated when he did as the man hacked down with his great saber. Percival swung his sword to give a counterstrike but the man parried. So began a number of strikes and parries from both fighters. The big man was strong but that was his only edge. Percival on the other hand may not have been as strong or as fast but he was smart. He saw the moves that they were both making as a game. It was all about strategy. His opponent wasn't thinking ahead. He was just doing what came to him naturally. Percival was seeing far ahead in the fight and knew that he could win. He anticipated a strike and brought his sword down to meet it. Then he feigned a fall. The brute did not fall for it. Percival then stood and put his hand in a pouch that was clasped to his belt. He charged forward, swinging his sword in what seemed to be random strokes. Each was blocked but then Percival made the man bring his sword low for a parry and when that happened, Percival threw a handful of broken glass into the man's eyes. It was a nasty trick that but it had been effective in the mortal world. Handfuls of tiny shards of glass would blind opponents and end their threats. Sure enough the man back away with a yell of confused pain. He dropped his sword and clasped a hand over his eyes. His hand was still there when Percival stabbed him.

The battle became chaotic. People were striking at each other from all directions. Shields were dented and swords battered until the blades were so dull they were little better than clubs. Yet they still fought, spears thrusting and swords swinging back and forth with little direction.

More minions joined the battle and when they did, magic was used abundantly. They may not have been the most skilled sorcerers but they knew how to cast deadly spells. One of the women on Percival's side was near one of the minions when he was casting a spell. She had a small knife in a sheath on her belt. She drew the knife and threw it. It lodge in the base of the minion's skull and stayed there until he turned to dust.

"Yes!" Percival yelled in triumph, nodding to the woman who had done the remarkable deed.

With another minion dead the battle seemed to be going all

right but then Percival heard a voice speaking into his mind. It was the cold, clear voice of Caltrin speaking to him. Percival listened to what was said and fear gripped his heart.

¤

Wulfric was victorious. Shouts of triumph echoed in the ruins of Riverbank. It was hard to believe that it had truly happened but it did. The large warband that had been led by General Tragor before his departure had been crushed by the rage of the rebels. Wulfric's people had fought in the most savage of ways and had filled the air with corpse-dust. Wulfric guessed that Serpintus had not suspected that they would win. Indeed, none of the surviving spearmen had believed they would win. The question of why Serpintus had withdrawn was obvious. He had seen the weapons forged from dark blade metal. Even though he could not really die and his body would begin reforming instantly, it was a great inconvenience and it hurt. It was also humiliating. No mere human could be allowed to obliterate Serpintus' body so the overlord had fled, taking his trusted men with him and believing those that remained would finish the rebel warbands.

Wulfric wondered how the others were doing. He hoped Percival was winning his battle but more than that he prayed to whatever God would listen that Caltrin and Barwick could make it to Arhanorgn untroubled.

Then, as he was thinking these things, another thought crossed his mind. This thought was not his own however. It was planted by a voice, Caltrin's voice. He had specific instructions for Wulfric. And just like Lord Percival, Wulfric felt fear in his heart.

¤

Serpintus was staring fixedly at the two travelers. They were flying but only a few feet off the ground so they would avoid detection. That hadn't worked. Serpintus saw the glowing blue globe that crowned Caltrin's scepter and felt a rush of excitement and anticipation. He was about face his enemy for the last time.

It had not been difficult for him to figure out what was truly happening with the rebels. The attacks had been so erratic that they may as well have announced themselves as distractions. Serpintus had gone into one of his chambers where he could see all of the Otherworld. There, in the midst of the desolation, he saw two people flying. He knew it was Caltrin and Barwick and so he gathered minions and General Tragor and his men and set off to stop his enemies.

"Where do you suppose they are going?" Tragor asked Serpintus as they watched.

"Wherever it is, I don't intend for them to reach it," Serpintus said softly.

From their vantage point they could see the two hurrying along the valley. Serpintus and his warband were well concealed by the mountains.

"Archers!" Serpintus called when Caltrin and Barwick were in range. "Fire!"

Arrows soared into the sky, fired by dozens or archers. Serpintus watched in expectation as the arrows either missed the magician or glanced off a dome shield he had suddenly created.

Serpintus then drew his sword and shouted, "Go!" When he did this, minions leapt into the air and dove to the valley below.

¤

Caltrin had created his shield just in time and the arrows had glanced harmlessly off the dome. He cursed under his breath. Serpintus knew where they were. That idea was confirmed when he saw the minions leap from one of the mountains and fly toward him. The magician counted eight of them and he prepared for a desperate fight.

"It may be time to call them," Caltrin said.

"They can't be transported when your magic is tied up," Barwick said as if Caltrin did not already know this.

"We need to get to cover," Caltrin said just before dropping the shield and delivering a magic blast to one of the minions.

Barwick gave out a war cry and drew his sword. He met one of the minions as the brute descended upon him. It was Harwain, champion of Serpintus and the minion who held the most power after Serpintus. It was a very brief fight. Harwain's sword clashed with Barwick's but then Harwain tried to kill Caltrin. Caltrin cast a shield-spell that simultaneously attacked Harwain and the minion fell over in surprise. Barwick stabbed him and sent his soul to the River.

"Go!" Barwick called to Caltrin. "I'll hold them off."

Caltrin nodded and ducked behind some rocks. While Barwick was fighting, he found a small cave where he could focus his powers. Placing the scepter against his forehead, Caltrin used his magic to link to the minds of Wulfric and Percival and prayed that they had not fallen.

"We have been found out," Caltrin said telepathically. "Bite into your capsules. We need you now."

As soon as he had sent his message, he rejoined the fight. He saw a mass of armored spearmen marching down the mountain and knew this would be a desperate fight and an even more desperate escape.

Caltrin saw an opportunity as he watched the spearmen marching down the mountain slope. While Barwick occupied the attacking minions, Caltrin shot a well-aimed charge of magic into the mountainside and caused a small avalanche. Spearmen cried out in pain, surprise ad fear as they were crushed by rocks. Most of the warband was still alive however but they were now halted, at least for a moment.

"Any time now, Percival," Caltrin said as he turned his attention to the minions.

Barwick was an expert fighter and he beat back two minions at the same time. A third had to join in the fight before he started to get overwhelmed. Caltrin joined in and they fought back to back.

"How far is Arhanorgn?" Caltrin asked Barwick.

"Not far," Barwick replied while parrying a blow. "The smaller mountain along this range is Arhanorgn. It's half a mile at most."

"Then we need to get there," Caltrin said.

Barwick did not reply. He was too focused on fighting. More minions were joining their comrades. Surprisingly however, Serpintus was not among them.

The enemy spearmen had begun making progress into the valley. Caltrin knew they would soon be overwhelmed.

Just as he was thinking this, a massive gust of wind blew through the valley. Soon another warband was there and this one was led by Wulfric. Armored men with spears, swords and shields had arrived, disoriented. They had to rely on their instincts and form a shield-wall to defend themselves against the minions. Percival and his men arrived moments later and swelled the numbers of Wulfric's men.

"Now!" Caltrin yelled.

He and Barwick then vanished. They couldn't have done this before since they would have been picked out and pursued. They were not totally invisible and their silhouettes could still be seen by anyone looking for them. Their spearmen would have to be the final distraction. And it worked. The minions and the enemy spearmen descending the mountain did not look for Barwick and Caltrin. They attacked the small army that had formed in the valley, believing that the two who had just vanished were waiting to make a surprise attack.

Percival and Wulfric's archers took aim at the minions and managed to hit a couple of them. Then the enemy spearmen made it to the valley. Now they were locked, shield-wall against shield-wall. The minions held back, not wanting to take the humiliation and pain of having their bodies destroyed.

Percival walked past his shield-wall with his sword in his hand. He wanted to make a formal challenge to a champion on the other side. This was customary in the mortal world and he had seen that the practice existed in the Otherworld. Now he came forward and threw down his shield. He said nothing. Standing in silence, he watched the enemy with contempt in his eyes. The enemy knew what he was doing without him strutting and dancing and spitting insults. Indeed, his silence and stillness was an insult. Finally, someone came forward to put an end to Percival's superior attitude. There was nothing overly remarkable about this man. He wasn't small or large, and there was nothing obviously threatening about him. Percival was relieved when this man came forward. This would prolong the conflict and that would give Caltrin and Barwick more time.

Percival pointed his sword at the man and the man responded by dropping his shield and spear and drawing his own sword. They then clashed their blades together as a sign that they agreed to the duel.

Percival knew this may be foolish. The minions could intervene and kill him while he was fighting the champion or the enemy spearmen could suddenly charge. Such an act would have been disgraceful in the mortal world but disgrace wasn't the same thing in the afterlife.

The enemy was the first to strike. He hacked at Percival but the blow was parried. Percival was now considering how foolish this challenge had been. He was tired from his other battle while before him stood a mass of fresh spearmen. Each had a spear and a sharp sword while Percival's sword was scarred, dented and dull; a thin, metal club.

The truth however was that he had no need to worry. His opponent was using brute strength, hoping to overpower the obviously tired Percival. Percival had a quick mind and he knew how to fight. It was not long after this unremarkable fighter showing displays of brute force met his end on Percival's blade. It happened in a flash. For a moment it had seemed that the man would kill Percival but then, Percival ducked a blow and kept moving until he had a shot at an exposed area in the man's defenses. Percival summoned as much strength a he could muster to drive the sword through the leather and flesh of his enemy and was crouching in the same position as the man turned to dust, his soul screaming in agony as it flew to its resting place on the River.

During the brief fight, both sides had been shouting support to their representative fighters and now only Percival's side was making noise while the enemy spearmen glared in stunned silence.

Percival knew that the enemy spearmen would consider charging the shield-wall and so he got back into the safety of the numbers. Once again the two shield-walls were frozen, each waiting for the other to make a move.

Percival was in command now. Wulfric had stepped aside when the former king's champion entered the battlefield and now he had to prove that he was still as good as he had been. He was getting ready to make the order to break the shield-wall. He was not afraid to do this, but he had a healthy respect for the danger and difficulty that was in breaking one.

Percival gave the order before the other side could. He decided that his best strategy was to break their wall. Even if they all fell to enemy spears they would at least distract them long enough for Barwick and Caltrin to make it to Arhanorgn.

It seemed a desperate gambit for the smaller army to attack Serpintus' mass numbers but that did not deter them. They charged and the sound of their spears and swords crashing onto shields and armor echoed through the mountains as a prayer to the Gods.

And on that day, the Gods heard them.

They were filled with an unnatural energy and strength that coursed through their bodies and drove them on to the kill. The enemy shield-wall was broken and the two armies were clashing in a mass of armor and blades. Corpse-dust filled the air and the screams of the souls echoed all around. Percival led his people to victory and on that battlefield in the valley, only his enemies fell.

¤

General Tragor knew that the battle was lost but that was not what was worrying him. He had not paid attention to the fight as his latest warband began forming into their shield-wall. He was scarcely aware of the duel between the champions but he didn't let it concern him. He wanted to know where Caltrin and Barwick were. Then, as Percival was leading the massacre of the overlord's soldiers, Tragor saw a flash of light not more than half a mile from where he stood.

"This way," he called to his horsemen who were mounted and waiting for orders. They had expected to join in on the battle below but the general had pointed to a small mountain not far away. He pointed at Arhanorgn.

The horsemen galloped toward the mountain. Serpintus, who was standing on a different plateau, saw the horsemen riding toward the mountain and knew that Tragor was onto something.

¤

Barwick and Caltrin had made it. They were inside of a cave that led deep into the heart of the small mountain. So much was riding on this mission that it seemed overwhelming but Caltrin did his best to think clearly.

"There is supposed to be a door right?" he asked Barwick.

The boatman was searching around frantically. He knew, as Caltrin did, that they only had a limited time before the minions discovered where they were.

"Yes," Barwick said. "It's called a doorway at least. Remember, when the Gods created this, they did not craft things the way we do. A door made by them may look completely different. It's supposed to call out to a magician."

It was then that Caltrin's scepter glowed red. The light from the scepter filled the cave and gave away their position to General Tragor. Eventually, the light receded into a sphere that traveled about the cave. It came to rest on circular indentation in the cave wall.

"That's the doorway?" Caltrin asked.

"I would assume so."

Then they heard the hoof beats of General Tragor's horsemen.

"I guess that had better be the door," Caltrin said. "We're out of time."

General Tragor dismounted and entered the cave on foot,

followed by his men. Julron was nervous of seeing Caltrin and Barwick again but attempted to show no sign of it. Yet his blatant defiance was evidence enough of his shame.

"Hello, Barwick," Tragor said. "It has been too long."

"Not long enough since I dumped your trashy soul in Riverbank," Barwick growled.

"That hurts, boatman. Now I must make you pay for that remark." The general then brandished a sword. "Do you know what this is?"

Barwick recognized it to be one of the swords forged in the Savage Land but said nothing.

"It's quite clever," Tragor said. "Forging swords with pieces of Dark Blade. It kills minions. Or at least sends them to the River where they wait to reform. Ingenious."

"I am glad you approve," Caltrin said.

"Oh my," Tragor said. "This was your idea? And here I thought you were about as clever as a rock. Maybe you still are and this was just a happy accident."

"I may only be clever as a rock but I defeated and humiliated that bastard Serpintus twice."

Tragor's face grew dark at the blatant disrespect for his lord. Time for talking and insults was over. It was time to kill.

"Kill them!" Tragor barked at his men.

Swords were drawn and the seven attacked. Barwick fought two at one time and killed them both. Caltrin, wanting to use as little magic as possible so he did not attract more unwanted attention, used his scepter as a club.

Things turned bad however. Barwick was stabbed. It was a lucky strike from a falling enemy but the blade was imbedded in his stomach. Barwick pulled it out and realized that it had not been a killing blow. He was severely weakened however. It would have been less painful just to have his current body destroyed and then reformed. Now he would have to spend his last moments in pain.

Tragor had also gotten lucky. He made Caltrin drop his scepter and when that happened, the magician lost his sight. Caltrin kept groping for the scepter and kept trying to summon it to him. But Tragor was bearing down on him and it seemed the magician would surely die.

Then, the final piece of the scheme designed by Norhan fell into place. The prophet had said that Tragor would be what would stop them from reaching Golgotha. He had also said he had taken care of that problem. Julron had survived the fight and was watching as General Tragor approached Caltrin. With a sudden flare of rage and hatred, not only for Tragor and Serpintus but also for himself, Julron stabbed the general from behind. Tragor felt the blade pierce the armor on his back and then pierce his skin. He felt it pass all the way though him until it stuck out through his chainmail and leather breastplate. Julron had screamed in triumph and hatred as he killed the general and he was still screaming as Tragor's body disintegrated and his soul went to its everlasting madness on the River.

Caltrin summoned his scepter again and this time it flew into his hands. His sight was immediately restored and he saw Julron standing with Tragor's armor skewered on his sword. There was no time to ask him why he had betrayed the general. He had to focus on Golgotha.

"Barwick!" he called.

"Here," the boatman replied.

"Let's go!"

Caltrin helped Barwick to his feet and then pointed the scepter at the circular indentation which was supposedly a door. He willed it to open and suddenly, he and Barwick were being sucked into a portal.

"The doorway," Barwick breathed as they passed through the opening.

¤

Serpintus had arrived just in time to see the doorway open. He was about to challenge Caltrin again but his eyes rested on Julron who was still standing. Furthermore there was armor draped on Julron's sword. Serpintus recognized it instantly as Tragor's armor.

"Traitor!" Serpintus raged. He slammed the boy against the cave wall and then wrapped his fingers around his throat. "That was my only friend. And you killed him. I am going to enjoy watching the life leave your eyes."

As Julron began to pass out from the lack of oxygen, Serpintus' attention was drawn from his revenge. The doorway was flashing brightly and the absence of the boatman and the magician told him that they had found a way to defeat him once and for all. He dropped Julron and ran for the door. He dove inside the circular portal and pursued his enemies to Golgotha.

Chapter Fourteen

The River of Souls runs through the mortal world but only the dead can see or enter it. Once a dead soul is in the Otherworld they cannot journey back to the mortal world for only the boatman can do that. He guards the mortal world from the dead and brings the dead to the afterlife.

Golgotha.

They had made it. Centuries after learning of where the minions could be destroyed, Barwick set eyes on the place where he would die. How remarkable, he thought, that after years of searching and guessing where the entrance could be, a prophet comes along (and through his actions brings forth the other two) and reveals the location.

How clever Norhan had been! He had seen what was to come and had found a path that he could take that would result in the death of the man who would have stopped them. That was why he demanded to go to Riverbank. It was so obvious now.

The journey through the portal seemed to take both an eternity and no time at all. And then they were in the Otherworld's small island in the mortal world.

From the island, Caltrin could see things that he remembered from his life. There were landmarks all around that he could see with his magically-heightened sight. There had been a time when he had ventured close to this island that was rumored to be a place of dead souls. Few mortals believed this was connected to the Otherworld but all agreed it was an evil place, filled with darkness. The dirt beneath Caltrin's feet was black as the obsidian rocks that littered the ground. There were dead trees with tattered cloth and ropes dangling from the branches. The sky overhead was a swirling black cloud. Caltrin remembered that black cloud and the unease he felt while looking at it. He felt the same unease now as he looked upon it once more. It looked exactly the same as he remembered it and he was sure that it had not changed in the decades since he had been there.

"This was created by the Dark Gods," Barwick said. "It was where They could go to be alone, Their domain so to speak."

"The Other Gods wouldn't come?"

"Eventually They did," Barwick said, "when the wars began. Before that though, They let the Dark Gods have a place for themselves. Part of what started the wars was what the Dark Gods did on this island."

"Which was?" Caltrin asked. Just as he did this he heard a wail of a woman in maddening pain. "What was that?"

"A remnant of what the Dark Gods did in this place."

Caltrin made light come from his scepter to see on the darkened island.

"Are you afraid?" Barwick asked.

"No," Caltrin lied.

They walked on until they came to what appeared to be a crater in the center of the island. It was a large hole at least thirty feet deep and just as many feet across. There was a staircase in the rock wall that led to the bottom.

"That is where we need to go," Barwick said.

"Clearly," Caltrin replied.

Caltrin sent a glowing orb of energy to the bottom so they could see what was down there. He gasped in disgust when he saw what was on the floor. It was a pile of bones and skulls that had been there for a long time.

"My Gods," Caltrin said.

"This is part of the reason that the Gods went to war. The Dark Gods tortured and killed humans and when the Other Gods found out They tried to punish Them. The struggle began. The minions were formed out of the death rituals on this island."

Barwick had shocked Caltrin by revealing this truth. He had never given any details about how the minions were created and no wonder. It was a disgusting way to be created and not something for which Barwick would have been proud.

"Come," Barwick said. "We need to finish this."

Barwick led the way to the bottom of the pit. Sure enough, there was an altar.

"At last," Barwick breathed a sigh of contentment. He was excited about ending his life and possibly redeeming himself in the process.

"I want you to know," Caltrin said, "that it was the greatest honor of my existence to serve under you."

"Thank you, Caltrin."

"I will miss you, my friend."

The boatman and the magician embraced like the old friends that they were. They had made it so far and had won and lost so much. Now it was the end.

Barwick broke the embrace and turned to the altar. It was made of stone and covered in dirt and bone fragments. Barwick brushed off the debris and sat on it.

"This is where I was born," he said.

For a moment neither said anything but then Barwick declared that it was time. "Serpintus might come through the door soon," he said, explaining the need to move faster.

"Very well," Caltrin said. He touched Barwick with the scepter and Barwick lay back on the altar. Caltrin then drew the dagger he had brought from the Savage Land. He gave his old friend a look that was intended to be the last look. He brought the dagger up to make the killing blow but then, just as he was beginning the stabbing motion, the dagger flew out of his hand. He turned and saw the dagger flying through the air, up to the ledge overlooking the pit, where Serpintus stood. The overlord caught the dagger in his hand and looked down on his two enemies with loathing.

"Damn," Caltrin said under his breath.

Without hesitation, the magician soared up to meet the overlord. He had to fight one last time and he had to win. The only thing that mattered was winning and getting that dagger back.

Serpintus drew his sword and hacked through the air creating a malicious spell aimed at Caltrin. Caltrin created a shield around his body that absorbed the spell and sent it back to Serpintus. Barwick joined the fight, using what little magic he could muster so far from the River.

"Clever of you," Serpintus said, "to find the location of my birthplace. Now we can continue where our Creators left off."

"You won't be killing anyone here," Caltrin said. It was purely wishful thinking on Caltrin's part but he spoke with the authority of someone who would make it happen.

Serpintus had to be careful not to kill Barwick for doing so may cause the required sacrifice to take place and so end the existence of the minions. He focused on killing Caltrin while deflecting any dangerous attacks from Barwick.

"What do you really think will happen?" Serpintus asked Caltrin. "You get rid of me and my brothers and sisters and then what? You think the Gods will return? You think They care a damn about you? You're smarter than that, Caltrin. You know that you will be on your own then."

"Then I will be on my own," Caltrin said. "But I will be rid of you."

Caltrin caused a small quake where Serpintus stood and forced the overlord to leap into flight to avoid falling. They fought ferociously, the wails of the island's dead echoing in the darkness.

Barwick was nowhere to be seen and that worried Serpintus but he had no time to think about it for Caltrin was fighting harder than ever. He had to focus all of his attention on beating the magician.

¤

Back in the cave, Percival and Wulfric were examining the portal. They had come not long after Serpintus had passed through the doorway and there they had found Julron who was barely conscious.

"Let me kill him," Wulfric said.

"No," Percival replied. "He will be our prisoner but we will not be killing him, at least not here."

"Why not?" Wulfric had demanded. "He is a traitor!"

"There is a reason that he is still here when no one else is," Percival said.

"Because he knows how slither out of danger," Wulfric said.

"Perhaps," Percival replied. "But I want to give him a trial at least."

The doorway was mesmerizing to Percival. He put his face up to the glowing blue portal and considered for a brief moment going forward. He checked himself however. As fascinating as the portal was, its destination was still unknown and that made Percival nervous.

"Do you think that they made it," Wulfric asked Percival.

"I hope so," Percival replied.

Then, as clearly as though they were fighting two feet away,

Percival heard the battle of magic occurring between Caltrin and Serpintus.

"No," Percival said.

"Damn," Wulfric said.

Percival and Wulfric looked at each other for a moment without speaking. They both knew what they needed to do and so Percival decided to do it first. He dove through the portal and traveled to Golgotha.

Wulfric watched Percival disappear into the small door and then prepared to do the same. He ordered his warband to follow him through the portal. But then, to his horror, the portal closed and Caltrin, Barwick, Percival and Serpintus were cut off from the Otherworld.

Percival appeared on the hellish island called Golgotha. He had been beckoned by Barwick who had been the one to amplify the sounds of the battle so that everyone in the cave could hear them.

As Percival stepped out of the portal, it closed behind him.

"No. No!," He saw Barwick standing there and asked: "Was that supposed to happen?"

"No, it wasn't," Barwick said with a bit of anxiety.

"Where's Caltrin?" Percival asked. He couldn't think about the door right now. He had to worry about the mission at hand.

"Come with me, Former Lord Percival," Barwick said.

Caltrin and Serpintus had progressed past the pit and were fighting on a rocky area of the island.

"Listen to me," Barwick said. "All that matters is that Caltrin kills me on the altar. Do you think you could distract Serpintus long enough for that to happen?"

"I think that I can," Percival said.

"Good. I wish I could fight but..." Barwick gestured at the wound on his stomach. "I can't do anything without the River and I'm cut off here."

"I understand," Percival said.

Percival crept along the rocks where the overlord and the magician were fighting their last battle. He was careful not to be seen. Caltrin was loosing, it seemed. He was holding most of Serpintus' attacks at bay but some were getting past his guard. His cloak was even more tattered than it had been before he had made it to the cave. He seemed weary now. It was obvious that Serpintus was on the verge of winning and killing Caltrin.

Percival took the knife made from dark blade out of its sheaf and waited on a rock for the best time to attack. He wished that he could get a message to Caltrin to let him know about the plan but he had to be content with hoping that Caltrin would take advantage of the chance Percival was going to give him.

Percival was on top of a boulder and as luck would have it, he got a shot at Serpintus. Caltrin had managed to land a spell that had knocked to overlord against a rock near Percival. Percival saw Serpintus get up and hover a few feet off the ground. He propelled himself forward and was about four feet from where Percival hid. Caltrin was coming back for another attack and Serpintus was waiting without any shielding to make himself an appealing target. Percival guessed that Serpintus had an evil trick up his sleeve and he would have been right. Then, as Caltrin began preparing the next attack, Percival leapt from the boulder. He had both hands on the hilt of the knife and he stabbed down as he descended onto Serpintus. The blade tore into Serpintus' cloak and into the cold flesh of his back. The overlord fell to the ground with Percival on top of him, howling in triumph.

Caltrin did not linger after he was given his one chance. He summoned the dagger from Serpintus' belt and flew through the air like an arrow. He saw Barwick and magically towed him toward the pit. They landed and Barwick ran back to the altar.

To Percival's horror Serpintus had not disintegrated. Instead, he rolled over with the force of a demon and picked up his own sword. He cornered Percival against the rock from which he had just leapt.

Caltrin killed Barwick. It was quick this time, no prolonged goodbye. Caltrin summoned all of his magic and coursed it through the dagger and then cut Barwick's throat. The boatman looked at Caltrin with tears of gratitude as his life ended. It was over. It was finally over.

Serpintus felt what had happened in his body and dropped his sword. Caltrin had won and the realization came to Serpintus accompanied by confusion. Caltrin couldn't win. He was human. The minions could not die. They could not fall. Just as he was thinking these things, his body began to break apart. It was not turning to dust like in the Otherworld. Serpintus was being destroyed and that meant his soul would not survive.

Caltrin watched as Barwick broke apart and Percival watched as Serpintus did the same thing. Both minions crumbled. There was a great flash of light emitting from both and then they were no more.

Serpintus was gone, no dust was left from him. He was gone, dead, finished.

As was Barwick.

Caltrin collapsed by the altar. He leaned against it and stayed there for a time. He sat in thought. It was hard to believe that it was over, that Serpintus and the minions were truly gone. But gone they were. After so many struggles and so much suffering, to achieve victory was nearly overwhelming. The magician reflected on these things while sitting by the altar, in the pit. That was where Percival found him.

"You did it, lord," Percival said when he had neared the bottom of the stairs.

"I did," Caltrin said. "We did. Barwick did." He then got to his feet and patted the stone top of the altar. Barwick's cloak and tunic were still hanging from it. "May you be at peace with yourself, my friend, if you still exist in any way."

Caltrin and Percival walked to the rock wall where the doorway had been. It was then that Percival explained how Barwick had summoned help and how the door had closed after Percival had come through, cutting him off from the rest of the army.

"So we are trapped here, it seems." Caltrin said.

"Can't you open it?" Percival asked, alarmed.

"I can't feel it," Caltrin said. He gave a attempt at opening the door but was unable. "I think you can only open it from the other side."

"Why would that be?"

"I don't know. There are a lot of things in the Otherworld that make no sense."

"Then how do we get back?"

"Don't worry," Caltrin said. "I've already thought of that."

Caltrin then led Percival to the island's shore. From there they looked out onto the black water and saw the shore of the mainland.

"Do you remember coming here?" Caltrin asked.

"One of your raids, I believe. I came back time and again after I became a lord. It always gave me the same uneasy feeling.

Mad howling began again but died away within seconds.

"The Dark Gods," Caltrin said, "were able to cross into the mortal world from right here. They brought people to this island to torture and kill them for their own amusement."

"That's monstrous."

"Granted," Caltrin said with a nod. "But it occurs to me, if the Dark Gods can enter the mortal world from here, why can't we?"

"And become ghosts? We need to get back to the Otherworld."

"The way I see it is that we are stuck here," Caltrin said. "Also, we are in our other-bodies. Therefore, if we set foot on the shore of the mortal world, we may see the River of Souls. From that river, we could find our way back to the Otherworld."

Percival thought about this for a moment. It seemed ludicrous and sensible all at once.

"What if the River doesn't appear," Percival asked.

"We're no worse off than we are now."

"Okay," Percival said. "Let's do it."

Caltrin leapt into the air, magically towing Percival behind him. As they approached the shore of the mainland the stormy sky became calmer. At last, when they reached the sands of the mainland, the sky was a clear blue. They could see Golgotha in the distance and the whirling black storm clouds overhead, but they were in the mortal world now, and they felt at home.

"I can't believe how much I love seeing a blue sky," Caltrin said.

"Me neither," Percival replied.

Then, just as Caltrin had predicted, wished and hoped, the River of Souls appeared. There was no boat for the boatman was now dead but the River was there and the River was their path to the Otherworld.

"Let's go," Caltrin said.

The magician leapt into the air once more with Percival. They flew across the River at a speed slower than Barwick's ships had gone. But the magic of the River had no master since Barwick was dead and Caltrin found that he could tap that magic. He channeled it through the scepter and was able to increase his flight speed. Within hours, they saw the ruins of Riverbank on the horizon.

"We will be welcomed back like heroes," Caltrin said.

"I suppose so," Percival replied.

"But I don't feel like a hero. I feel like a murderer."

The surviving members of the army saw their approach. They had gathered in Riverbank after the battle and were discussing the best way to cross to the Savage Land, where their homes waited. Percival and Caltrin landed in Riverbank and there they were greeted by applause.

In the days after, the story was recounted how Wulfric had watched the door collapse behind Percival and was unable to help. Not long after that happened, the minions who had been cut down during the battle had returned and the battle resumed. This time, the minions were not so arrogant and they were able to hold their own against the scattered spearmen. But relief was felt when the minions were obliterated. When that happened, all knew that Caltrin and Barwick had defeated Serpintus. They knew that the minions were defeated and gone forever.

There was much mourning and sorrow when Caltrin relayed the tale of how the minions were truly defeated. He explained the magic involved in the creation of the minions and what was required to destroy them. He revealed that it had been Barwick's intention all along to sacrifice himself to get rid of Serpintus and that Caltrin had known he would have to do it.

Caltrin, after recovering from all of the magic that he had used, flew across the sea and brought Lord Hullsham from the Savage Land. Temporary shelters had been erected outside of Riverbank and guards had been set to watch for human followers of Serpintus who may still linger. Hullsham was given the largest of the tents in the camp.

"We are going to have to conquer," Hullsham said to the people a few days after being brought from the Savage Land. "This is a large land without order. We can do it though. We can remake the Otherworld in hopes that our Gods may return."

Wulfric had been returned to the Savage Land to keep the villages under control until more reliable transportation could be arranged. Therefore, Wulfric had no say in Julron's fate. The traitorous boy was brought before Hullsham, Caltrin and Percival and those three deliberated on what to do with him.

"Is it true," Percival said, "that you turned against the former overlord's army?"

"Yes it is, lord," Julron said.

"You killed General Tragor," Caltrin said. "I saw you do it."

"I had to do it, lord," Julron replied. "I had seen too many horrible things and had done too many horrible things on that man's orders. I know that it is not enough to make up for my sins, but for a moment, I stepped in the right direction."

"Listen to me," Caltrin said. "We will not be trusting you lightly."

"Nor do I expect you to," Julron replied.

"There is something you can do for redemption," Caltrin said. "I have spoken with Lords Percival and Hullsham and they both agree with me. The thing is, what you can do comes with a great wealth of power. But this power chooses those who are pure of heart. It will not allow you to use it if you cannot be trusted."

"But you just said that I can't be trusted."

Hullsham spoke for the first time. "The power will prove whether or not you can be trusted. If you are interested in redemption you may have a chance at it. If not, leave our sight and never return. We will let you go as a reward for killing Tragor but banish you as punishment for joining him in the first place."

"I will do anything to clear my soul," Julron said.

"Very well," Hullsham said. "Go to the River. We will be watching."

Julron then realized what was being asked of him. He felt greatly honored and humbled at the same time. He was to take Barwick's place if the River allowed it. He knew there could be redemption there and so he obeyed and left the tent. He walked the few miles to the River and stood on the edge.

"Just wade in," Caltrin said. He did not have to tell Julron this though. The boy could feel what to do. He stepped into the water and felt a surge of energy through his body. He walked further in and then dove underwater. He was under for minutes and then he emerged further from the shore. Those watching saw that he was being elevated higher and higher out of the water. They saw that a wooden platform was beneath him. But it wasn't a wooden platform. It was part of a ship. The ship came out of the water with Julron on top of it.

"I think that it has chosen me!" Julron called to the shore.

Caltrin nodded solemnly while Percival smiled. Hullsham remained impassive.

"Now that that's settled," Hullsham said, "we have other work to do."

He led Caltrin and Percival back to the tent. There they planned out the conquering crusade that would begin when they had amassed their full strength. Hullsham did not want to leave things to chance. This campaign would be thought out and executed properly. His throne was at stake here and he wanted to make sure he was acclaimed king when it was all over. He would remake the Otherworld but whether the Gods returned or not was not important to him. He wanted to recreate paradise and he could only do that after a swift crusade that would put all of the Otherworld under his power. Caltrin and Percival drafted strategies and revised details relentlessly. All three men had different reasons for what they were doing. Hullsham wanted to rule. Caltrin wanted to protect. Percival wanted to retire.

At the end, they may all get what they want but for now they must focus on what's next, the crusade and the rebuilding of the Otherworld.

CPSIA information can be obtained at www.ICGtesting.com
Printed in the USA
BVOW042303200911

271699BV00003B/1/P

9 781612 960579